HOT LIVING

HOT LIVING

Erotic Stories About Safer Sex

John Preston, editor

Boston · Alyson Publications, Inc.

This is a paperback original from Alyson Publications, Inc.,
PO Box 2783, Boston, MA 02208.
Distributed in England by GMP Publishers,
PO Box 247, London, N15 6RW.

First edition, July 1985 5 4 3 2 1

ISBN 0 932870 85 6

Contents

To Richard Umans

Richard Umans had hoped to contribute to this volume. He died of AIDS on February 11, 1985, before he could complete his story. This book is dedicated to him, a fine writer with a firm vision, whose great talent has been denied us all by this modern-day plague.

The writers and editor of this book have received only a small payment for their work in recognition of their professionalism. All future royalties from *Hot Living* will be given to the Gay Men's Health Crisis. We strongly urge you to support this important undertaking and the many other organizations in the gay community that are working so very hard to respond to the health crisis.

If you would like to make a contribution to GMHC, your tax-deductible donation should be sent to: Gay Men's Health Crisis, Box 274, 132 West 24 Street, New York, New York, 10011.

Introduction

JOHN PRESTON

At the most basic level, the purpose of pornography is to produce masturbation. Its critics go to another extreme, they claim pornography's function is to act as propaganda for sexual exploitation in its most despicable forms.

I've always felt that erotic fiction does have a role in education. I've long believed that it is used as a means of sex instruction by gay men. What would this act feel like? How would this fantasy take form? Why might I accomplish this exploit? Erotica helps us answers these questions.

My own acknowledgement of pornography as a means of self-education doesn't take me to the extreme of the anti-erotica perspective. What's involved in my definition and missing in the others, for instance, is a belief that the individual is clearly responsible for the choices of what he or she reads, and for how she or he acts after the reading, and that all of it is involved with the predispositions that the person brings to erotic fiction.

The idea that pornography – or any other kind of fiction – can create behavior by itself is ludicrous once one looks at the effects of other types of writing.

I contribute a regular column of opinion to a Boston-based gay and lesbian newspaper, *Bay Windows*. For over two years I have demanded that people be more public about their sexuality, that they support and contribute to gay organizations as a matter of great importance, that they educate themselves about the numerous important aspects of AIDS, that they become politically involved, that they . . .

In those two years, sad to say, hardly anyone's come out because of my exhortations; gay organizations continue to be underfinanced; AIDS education isn't close to being done by enough people; few new voices have been heard in the gay political process . . .

That is not to say that those columns are useless. What my ideas – whether they be non-fiction political opinions or erotic fantasies – accomplish when I give them the substance of print is to help people make choices. My writings, fiction or not, open options, display dilemmas, and, I would imagine, often give form to ill-defined sets of expectations, hopes and desires.

Over the last couple years the health crisis that has devastated the gay male community has produced a growing awareness of a new set of needs. As the sparse knowledge about AIDS and its characteristics has begun to become more concrete – and it has only begun to do so – we gay men have been faced with a series of literally life-protecting choices.

While a cloud of mystery still hangs over much about AIDS, there is little doubt that the deadly disease is transmitted by intimate sexual contact. Just how, just when, just why, is still not defined. But the vast majority of material on AIDS suggests that there is a definite increase in "risk" involved in some sex acts. Nearly all researchers believe that we gay men can reduce that risk by altering our sexual habits.

From this came the concept of "sensible sex." Gay organizations around the country, medical personnel and others have spent enormous amounts of energy to promote these practices. They have been remarkably successful. For instance, numerous studies of the rate of venereal disease among the gay male population in vaious cities show significant decrease in its occurence. Since the practice of sensible sex is absolutely a means to reduce the spread of those diseases, it's obvious that lots of gay men have been taking steps that reduced their exposure to VD.

But there's been a problem.

Everyone insisted that sensible sex was *boring*. It had to be; it was good for you . . . but there was a sense that it was insufficient, that to practice it was a form of denial, not of celebration. Here is an example of what I call the "predispositions" of people coming to the fore. I think that gay men want to have a good time; I think they want to practice responsible sex for themselves and for the sake of the men they love.

I was very aware of these factors when Sasha Alyson approached me with the idea of doing a book that could respond to our needs in this health crisis. We talked over various options. Alyson Publications will be following through on others, but this volume is the place where I felt I could work most effectively.

We agreed that I would approach a number of writers and ask each for a story which would eroticize responsible sex. We wanted to get together stories that would perform the functions that I ascribe to pornography. We wanted fiction that would help make it possible for readers to see how new sexual situations could be desirable, not just necessary.

The writers who were asked to participate in the project responded enthusiastically. There is a very real sense that this is one of those books that's happened at the perfect time of ripeness. If I was right to speculate that gay men would like to read this volume in order to bolster their personal commitments to sensible sex, I was absolutely right to think that a group of the major writers of erotic gay fiction wanted to provide the opportunity.

I need to be very clear about the idea of safer sex, especially as it's portrayed in this book. As I approached the topic I spent a great deal of time with many people who I have worked with in various community educational projects about AIDS. I certainly had those conversations with many people who have labored in the major cities where — so far — most of the AIDS cases and AIDS concern have taken place. I talked with the (too many, far too many) people I know who've contracted the disease. I read as much as I could of the volumes of literature that have been produced by organizations such as the Gay Men's Health Crisis, the National Gay Task Force, and other local, regional and national groups.

The amount of material is awesome, so are the number of opinions. Everyone wants to support risk reduction during this health crisis, yet there is no real agreement just how to do that the "right way."

In the end, the long and thoughtful conversations I had with people here in Maine produced the final definitions that I've used and which I gave to the contributors. In particular, Miles Rightmire of the Gay Health Action Committee, Phil Gautreau of the Gay People's Alliance and Albert Nickerson of the Maine Health Foundation helped me shape this very basic definition.

Those three men are not responsible for my final decisions, but in our conversations we were able to share some perceptions of what was happening in our attempts to educate our own community here in Maine and what we saw happening in other places. I think it's important for you to understand those observations and analyses:

When AIDS was first defined and diagnoses first began to come to public attention, most often in highly sensationalized ways, the immediate response of many medical people was to insist that gay men had to stop having sex with one another in order to stop their exposure. If I had taken the most drastic forms of risk reduction suggested by some medical personnel even today, this would be a book about men standing in corners masturbating.

There are a number of questions about how AIDS is transmitted. Can it be carried in saliva? If so, kissing is out. Is any cock sucking at all a major risk or is it really a question of swallowing semen? Is any fucking bad; is there such trauma to the walls of the rectum that it is automatically going to produce a state where AIDS will be more likely?

At first, it seemed that all decisions should err on the side of safety. Even sweat is suspect, so no licking of body parts. When these were given to a community of men the results that we saw were that the prohibitions were so severe, the danger was so emphasized, that people threw their hands up in the air and stopped listening. The precautions that were being prescribed were too much for people to see as realistic guidelines by which to live our lives.

There is a nagging thing about all this; it presents a distressful dilemma. Almost none of the prohibitions is *known* to be necessary. They are guesses, some much better than others.

As a means of public education, we knew that the first set of guidelines couldn't work. But we also know that sensible sex was still very important to the gay male population. We had to give out realistic means of risk reduction that people would use to protect their lives. Here, as a bottom line, is the definition of safe sex that we constructed:

Do not ingest semen in any form. You can touch a cock, even with your mouth, but do not swallow the semen. Researcher tell us that this will decrease risk greatly. But there are questions that haven't been answered; you should realize that there may be risk in any oral-genital contact. Some people point to the fact that many men seep seminal fluid as soon as they're aroused. Does pre-cum pose such a risk that we shouldn't take the chance? Still others, at the other end of the spectrum, say that taking cum in your mouth might be all right, if you spit it out.

There can be no oral-anal contact. There is no doubt that rimming is a highly effective way to transmit disease. There is a great deal of informed speculation that AIDS is very similar to hepatitis in many ways. Certainly, rimming is the fastest way to transmit that disease as well.

Don't fuck without a condom. Fucking without a rubber is a means of ingesting semen. The dangers involved are too great at this time.

Do not swallow urine.

If these guidelines are follwed, the risk of transmitting a whole list of diseases would be greatly decreased. AIDS is not the only deadly one; we've treated hepatitis as though it were the common cold for far too long.

Those, then, are the guidelines given to writers in this volume. I'm responsible for them; some will argue with them; they are the ones I believe most realistic for us to use.

But the recommendations on how gay men should go about having sex these days aren't just limited to sexual acts. It is not the number of sexual acts that defines risk, it is the number of sexual partners. Having sex 100 times with one partner is not the same as having sex with 100 different men, once each.

The stories are meant to encourage a more limited number of partners, especially to discourage anonymous ones. Here came an incredible problem. There is a feeling going around in the world that romance is the only answer; love will conquer the disease. *It will not.*

How, though, can the stories in this book address that? Of course, one way to reduce risk is to limit oneself to a single sex partner. But the idea is that if sex takes place only with that lover then sensible sex needn't be practiced. *That's not true.* No one knows enough about the life characteristics of the disease. We do know that the incubation period – the time span between exposure to the disease and its manifestation – can be as long as five years. We do not know at what point it's communicable. There is a desperate desire to believe that if one takes a lover and is monogamous for a year, then everything will be okay. I'm sorry; that is no guarantee.

Many of these stories are shot full with love and romance. Please do not misinterpret that. I do not believe that these writers agree that monogamy is the most desired form of sexual union, nor that full-flown limerence is always a desirable state.

There is still another point about the way in which we gay men approach sex. This is something that became very clear to Sasha Alyson and me as we worked on the project. If we are to seriously examine how we have sex and what the repercussions of it are, we also need to look at some of the personal perceptions we have about sex. Most essential: Is it necessary to have *penetration?* What does that mean to us? Must fucking be the central sex act? Is sex insufficient if fucking doesn't occur?

The cheapest and easiest form of pornography is to describe a character being plowed by a mammoth cock, being split open by a huge tool, being . . . But it's not necessary. The stories in this book are very consciously presenting you with perceptions of sex that don't require fucking and, where fucking is shown, they do not display aggressive fucking. That's on purpose.

But let's go on to the good parts.

In this volume are contributions by some of the best known gay writers today. They include a huge variety of styles, some are part of the gay literati, many have published books, some are the best known pornographers in the country. They've come together here to give you one very essential message: Sex is not over with. There are ways to have sex that are enjoyable, and that are desirable.

The contributors to this book have worked hard to deliver this message to you. But, again, it's a question of your own predispositions. It is up to you to decide to act responsibly. We can only suggest the various ways that that is possible.

This volume is certainly not inclusive. You certainly still have many other options. There's a lot to play with here; there's more in your head. There are fantasies to explore and there are games to play with a sense of joy. Sex has always been a special means of communication and self-affirmation for gay men. The idea that it was going to be denied us by AIDS was one of the greatest concerns we had. It was no simple question about celibacy, it was a question of one of our means of life affirmation being stolen from us.

We were in a psychic winter. Our mourning, residues of our socially enforced guilt, and our fear, all produced a sense of despair when the AIDS crisis began. The crisis is far from over. But we can be better prepared to answer the crisis if we can regain some of the sense of empowerment and validation that sex gives us. That's the purpose of this book.

It's up to you how to use it.

John Preston
Portland, Maine
March, 1985

The Broken Vessel

PHIL ANDROS

His name was Salvatore Rossini, and I had known him for a long time, really, before the accident and of course after. He was one of those "white" Italians, not the swarthy darker kind, and his body had always made me think of some sculpted statue of Apollo, one that had been lost for uncounted ages and finally discovered at some archeologist's dig in Sicily. It had the beauty of line that was purely classical, from the square pectorals down the rugged belly to the ligament that swooped down to pass under his cock and balls and up the other side, like the torso of a faun by Praxiteles.

Back in the early days of our acquaintance he had been a hustler like me, a kind of mixed-up kid from a poor family. He hustled because he had to, for the money, not because he enjoyed it. We were always running into each other, as we made the "circuit" from Miami to Dallas, to L.A. and up to San Francisco and then Chicago and New York, and starting all over again. We occasionally fell into bed with each other when business was bad and there wasn't anything else to do and we were hot enough – or really cold and bored and just wanted our rocks off or asses hauled or whatever the case might be. I'm sure we both looked on our encounters as just a necessary thing, certainly not romantic, never getting us involved with each other – and never mentioned to anyone else, because it sure as hell would have played hob with our reputation as hustlers, doing it for nothing and just because we were momentarily heated up or the nights were cold or the clients were scarce.

But I liked Sal and I guess he liked me, and we formed a kind of Greco-Italian alliance. We were hesitant in those days about spoiling our "image" in each other's eyes, or maybe we were each thinking that word might get out to the circle of clients, and we'd be spoiled as macho hustlers. At any rate, oddly enough we were sort of shy with each other — maybe not so shy as just pretending to want to get it over with in a hurry . . .

"Sheez, I'm hot tonight," I might say. "Gimme a hand-job."

Or: "Do me a little tit-work," he'd say, "while I beat my meat."

Imagine! After all we'd done, maybe earlier during that same day! It was almost as wicked as two little boys up in the hayloft in Grandpaw's barn, trying some early experiments. All that was lacking was measuring each other's dingdongs for size, but we didn't do that because by then the built-in yardstick we had each developed in our eyes told us that we were approximately the same length. Eight or nine maybe, and what's an inch between friends? But I'd never known anyone as sensitive around nipples and armpits as he was. Just touching his right nipple — his trigger he called it — sent a wave over him of what the French call a *frisson* — a real chill that raised every pore on his chest-skin and sent a small ripple through all the muscles of his torso. You could see that frisson travel across the ridges and valleys of his stomach muscles, up to his left armpit and then down towards his man-sized cock. It was like watching a miniature earthquake tumbling across his flesh.

A coupla years ago we lost touch with each other, and not being the letter-writing kind, either of us, I didn't know where he was or what had happened to him. Then last summer I ran into a former client, Bill Broderick, the gay professor who had given up teaching English in the university to become "secretary" to one of the Mafia lawyers on whom Bill had earlier had a case. We met on a hot evening in Chicago in the Drake hotel bar looking out on the darkening expanse of Lake Michigan where a lake breeze had stirred up a few whitecaps on the black water.

Someone touched me on the shoulder while I was absently

turning the stem of my martini glass. "Phil," he said.

I turned around. It was Bill, all right – looking a little older but not much, that thin pencil moustache of his just a bit touched with grey, sideburns too, and wearing an elegant and expensive dark blue suit.

"Damn," he said, "after all these years. And what the hell are you doing in a suit and looking like an executive on his night out?"

His handshake was firm and strong. "As I live and breathe,' I said with my characteristic originality, "it's the old English teacher."

He slid, grinning, onto the stool next to mine. "How long has it been?"

"Long enough," I said. I liked Bill, and our lives at one time had been woven so close together over the lanky handsome Luigi di Lupo who for a while owned the northside bar called Sans Souci. I had been indirectly responsible for Bill's finding out that his macho idol, Luigi, had really been diddling at two-backed beast with me. And out of that discovery had come Bill's happy departure from academe and his landing in the office – and bed – of Luigi. It was one of the few times in my life when I had played Cupid instead of being just an ordinary pimp.

We fell to talking about the old days and the people we had known.

"Still with your adored italiano?" I asked.

"Sure," said Bill. "You know I like anything that comes out of the boot."

"The boot?" I asked, puzzled. "You a foot man now?"

"Not exclusively," he said, grinning. "I meant, the shape of Italy. Looks like a boot, you asshole."

"Oh yeah," I said, somewhat miffed at my failure to catch his reference. "Me too. I like 'em all."

"Did you ever know a guy named Sal Rossini?" Bill asked. "Seems to me I heard him mention your name once."

I had a sudden warm feeling. "Sure, I knew him," I said. "Good ole Sal. How's he doin' nowadays?"

Bill stopped smiling. "Oh, you haven't heard," he said.

"Something wrong?"

"Yes," Bill said. "About a year or two ago he had an accident."

"Serious?" I said.

"Yes. You know how damned good-looking he was – beautiful. Like a statue by Bernini. Or Michelangelo."

"What happened?"

"Well, he got hooked on motorcycles, and –"

I groaned. "Murdercycles, you mean. At least that's what Pete Swallow used to call 'em."

"Luckily it didn't go quite that far," Bill said. "But it might as well have. He lost both legs and the use of one arm. Partially paralyzed. Lives up on Glenwood now in a small apartment. A nurse comes in once a day. But he's got no feeling below his belly button. He can feed himself and he's as bright as ever. Even exercises with some weights. But it's bed and the wheelchair from now on for him. That and TV and reading. I go see him about once a week if I can."

"Ah *shit*!" I said violently. "And he's only about thirty." I paused. "What a heluva life. What's he do for sex?"

Bill looked disturbed. "I tried at first to help him out," he said. "Tried masturbating him. But that didn't do any good – no feeling at all in his cock."

Back in some dim cavern of my mind I felt something stir – an old memory of something I'd seen somewhere while reading Kinsey years ago. I couldn't drag it out into daylight, but it kept tickling me . . .

"You got his address and phone number?" I said to Bill. "How's about my going up to see him?"

Bill took out a pencil and wrote on the inside of a matchbook cover and gave it to me. I stuck it away. We talked some more – a lot more.

"You still hustlin'?" he asked finally.

"Yeah," I said. "Not too much any more. Everybody's scared nowadays. So'm I. It's the new lifestyle."

"Yeah," said Bill. "I stay pretty close myself. Luigi's enough for me."

"He'd be enough for anyone," I said, grinning, "from what I remember about his size."

"You going to be around town long?"

"For a while," I said. "I've got a room."

"Gimme your address," Bill said, and I did.

And then somehow the evening and the talk petered out. Bill stayed another few minutes and left – had to get home, he said. I had one more drink after he had gone, and then I left too. Night had come, the time when I should come alive, but somehow that evening I didn't feel much like it. The news about Sal had set up a melancholy in me that drained the beauty out of the night, and left me feeling ready for nothing except home and bed and sleep, and perhaps the calm that always followed, like a reward, the pleasure of my hand upon myself.

\+ + + + + + +

I'd looked often enough deep inside myself to see if I could find the reason for my liking what I called the "broken vessels" – guys who were incomplete, who had lost something or other . . . an eye, an arm, a leg. Maybe it was because of some deep-rooted residual feeling about the incompleteness of myself, my own incompleteness maybe, as – for an extreme instance – for my not liking women – wholly unconscious and incapable of being brought to the surface where I could look at it. I remembered Bill Gibson, and my fascination with his right arm. It was not finished – somehow in the mysterious alchemy of the womb his right arm lacked the hand, and his forearm became a kind of lengthy tapered cock, very good for fisting – and he was in great demand for that, although he didn't care for it at all. And there were others, from Vietnam and elsewhere – a guy with an eyepatch who made me think of pirates and ads for Hathaway shirts. And I remembered the first guy I'd been to bed with who had only one leg. The smoothness of the stump was something I couldn't take my eyes from, and of course it made screwing him easier – no leg in the way. Deep down there was powerful sympathy in me for these broken vessels – and often they seemed a lot more intriguing than the perfect bodies. This, I decided, was perhaps the really most bizarre thing in my entire makeup, and I never discussed it with anyone.

The next afternoon was golden and autumnal, and when Chicago has nice days they really can compare with the best ones in any part of the world. The air was soft and gentle, and the small breeze from the lake tousled my hair. I took the elevated up to Argyle station, and gradually found my way to the address that Bill Broderick had given me. It was a small yellow house with a concrete ramp leading up to the door – for a wheelchair, I supposed.

I rang the bell. From somewhere I heard Sal call out: "I'm around back, come on!"

So I picked my way around the side of the house to a tiny backyard. There was a kind of arbor there – yes, by gum, a grape arbor! I hadn't seen one of those in twenty years, with the broad flat leaves climbing over the top of it and the sun making a dappled pattern of green and gold light on what lay beneath.

And there was Sal. He was sitting in an ordinary chair with a thin blanket over his lower body, his torso naked. He had found the only patch of sunlight that let the rays fall entirely on his upper body. The covering was pulled up to his crotch where some pubic hair showed, and I looked briefly at the flat emptiness where his legs should have been.

"Phil, ole buddy!" he said, and extended his right arm and hand. His left lay motionless on the chair arm. "Damn, I'm glad to see you!"

I shook his hand. The grip was strong, the skin lightly moist and warm.

"You've had some bad luck," I said, a little embarrassed.

"Yep," he said. "But nuthin' I can't live with. I manage. It's been nearly two years."

"You're used to it now?" It was inflected like half a question.

"Sure thing. I get around the house all right. 'Course I don't go hustlin' any more, but sometimes they come to me."

"For sex?" I said in amazement. "Or is it just . . . pity?"

He shrugged. "I still give a good hand job," he said. "With grease," he added, grinning.

"You're still the same goodlooking' stud," I said.

And he was. The black curly hair lay in good waves on his head, the eyebrows were full and down-pointed at the ends, his nose was thin and perfect above the deep red fully-carved lips that looked as if they had been constructed to fit around a cock, and in his strong chin there was the deep cleft that I had always envied. His eyes were bright blue – piercing, I suppose you'd call them – steady and shining. And his torso! Bronzed deep sienna by the sun, with square pectorals and a small sprinkling of hair, the moist and sweaty ridges of his abdomen above his tucked-in navel, the black hair heavy in his armpits, and the remarkable bulge of his right biceps and triceps. I noticed a ten-pound barbell lying on the ground beside him – one of the oldfashioned kind of dull iron with a spherical ball at each end – not the shining new chrome cylinders you see nowadays.

"Man, you look as if you're in top condition," I said.

"Exercise every day," he said, picking up the barbell. "I could arm wrestle you down in ten seconds flat."

"I don't doubt it in the least, with an arm big as that," I said.

We fell to talking . . . about old scores and places, the details of his accident, the people he still knew – and the ones I knew along with him. His talk was animated – and certainly not the complaining sort of whine you might have expected from one in his position. He told me how well he got around, about his motorized wheelchair, how he went to the grocery down the block, and all the rest. We talked about Bill Broderick and Luigi – whom he had also tricked with. It was like a meeting of housewives over the backyard fence, full of gossip and good humor and many laughs. And then finally, as you might expect, we got around to sex.

"And just what do you do for it?" I asked.

He made a wry face. "Mostly I have to depend on wet dreams," he said. "But they come often and they're real fine. Everything happens just as it's 'sposed to, and I can even sometimes make the people do what I like – make 'em go down on me, or let me fuck them. It's great. The only trouble is they don't happen all that often. I've got no feeling at all below my belly-button so I can't jack off – although when I'm dreamin' I usually have a stinkin' hardon and feel it fine. Phantom feelings the doc calls 'em. But while I'm asleep I've still got my big dick."

It was just at that moment that the rusty drawer in the back of my head popped open – a drawer I hadn't looked into in twenty years. I remembered something – probably from my reading Kinsey all those years ago.

"Say," I said, "how's your imagination . . . your fantasy mechanisms?"

"First-rate," he said. "I keep goin' over all my past scores and even though I can't feel anything they can sometimes raise my cock up to its full height. What didja use to call yours – old Betsy? Mine's still rarin' to go once in a while, even though I can't feel a thing."

"I've got an idea," I said. "But a lot depends on you. Where's your sensitivity line exactly?"

He looked puzzled. Then he reached over to a little table beside him and picked up a small instrument. It had a chrome handle with a forty-five degree bend in it, and at the end a little metal wheel, with tiny sharp points at the end of its many spokes.

"The doc gave me this. I test myself every once in a while, run it over my body to see if I can feel any more than I did. My line just now goes from the middle of my ribs on the left side down to my right hipbone."

"So that includes both nipples?" I asked.

"Yeah," he said.

The rusty drawer began to spill out its contents. A plan formed. "I've got an idea," I said.

"What's that?"

"Tell you sumpin, ole buddy. You just lie back and shut your eyes, and think of the most sexy person you ever had."

"You, maybe? Or who? What's goin' on?" he said.

"Just do what I said." I took off my jacket and T-shirt.

He did. His torso gleamed in the sun, and his thick black eyelashes lay closed on his cheeks. What pictures were being projected on the screen of his imagination I had no way of knowing.

I didn't know quite how to begin. I started with his face, drawing the backs of my fingers down his jawline, first on one side and then the other, then gently playing with his ears a little, letting my fingers trace around the shells of them, and dipping a little into the porches. Then his eyes and eyelids — they quivered. And then his nose, and at last his mouth, tracing the deep curves of his red lips and gently putting my finger inside them, and then the cleft in his chin, finally going to the sides of his neck, stroking, stroking, the hollow at the base of his throat, and then the cheeks again. From there I slid softly to his upper chest, letting my fingers drift slowly over it, and finally slipping down to his nipples. Gently I took one between thumb and forefinger, rolling it until it hardened, and then squeezing it firmly and gripping it and pulling it outward.

He was not motionless. His head was turning from side to side, and a faint sigh came from his lips. I lifted the covering over his cock; it was about half hard, in that heavy stage when it seems to weigh a coupla pounds. It lay over against his left leg, and as I fingered his nipples, especially his right one, it jerked a little.

Then the frisson began — a small convulsive ridge that traveled from his right hip up towards his left armpit, a small ridge marked by moving chill-specks. His sighing changed to breathing, at first rapid and then becoming hard. I bent over that handsome torso and took his left nipple in my lips, sucking and rolling it between them, thudding it with my tongue. And then I moved to his right one — his trigger, as I remembered — concentrating on it, sucking, pulling with my lips and gently biting it with my teeth, and taking the whole area into my mouth. My hands were by now roving over that whole magnificent torso, feverishly, clutching the back of his neck as well. I tongued his navel, and then using my whole tongue flattened, I licked the faint salt of his sweat up and around his whole belly, rising to his right armpit and its abundant hair, biting the strands a bit, and moving on to the left one, more strongly and excitingly musky.

I raised my head and looked at his cock. It was engorged, red, and throbbing. I returned to my labors, licking, sucking his nipples, using my hands on his face and neck and throat and back of the head and belly, and then finally clasping him strongly to my own naked torso, burying my head against his neck and licking his ear. His right arm pressed me hard against his chest.

His breathing had grown shorter. He was panting — strong gusts in and out of his mouth and nostrils. I raised my head again to look at his face – saw the eyes squeezed tight and the mouth squared off . . .

And then I looked at his cock. It had risen to its full height and size, and as I watched I saw the white gyzym spill forth – not in spurts but in a slow stream that rose a little and then ran down the side of his cock. His body strained against mine and convulsed. Then he shuddered. The strength went suddenly away and he collapsed in my arms.

He was still panting. Gradually his breathing slowed and at last he opened his eyes.

"Gah-damn," he swore softly. "It r-really happened. . . ."

"Sure did, ole cock," I said. I pulled some kleenex from the nearby box and wiped him up.

"How could a thing like that happen? I actually felt the sensation in my cock."

"Phantom feelings," I said. "I read about it somewhere once. Husband had been in an accident, and the wife learned how to bring him to climax and shoot just by caressing him."

He shook his head. "It's a miracle," he said.

I punched him on the shoulder. "No way," I said. "Just some foreplay. Now you finally know it can happen, you're gonna have fun."

"Who could I get to make love to me that way?" he asked.

I shrugged. "Lotsa people. Me, for one. I'm gonna be here for about another month. And then there's Bill Broderick. I'll tell him how it's done if you want me to."

"I sure as hell do," he said, his whole face glowing with a new light. "But maybe you'll come back soon?"

"Sure thing," I said. "How's about next Wednesday, same time?"

"I'll save it up for you," he said, grinning.

I put on my T-shirt and jacket. "Until then," I said, beginning to move away.

He looked as if he wanted to say something. I paused. Then he did.

"You . . . fucker," he said, grinning. "You beautiful . . . gah-damned fucker."

Friends

TOBY JOHNSON

"These days one needs to be discriminating about how and with whom you have sex," my friend Steve and I were agreeing over a late dinner at San Francisco's Hamburger Mary's. We were talking about changes in gay life as a result of the health crisis.

Neither of us was "promiscuous" – at least not in the way that word was usually used in the AIDS literature. But that didn't mean we didn't enjoy and seek sex or didn't long for the feel of a man in our arms. It did mean we were both conscious of the techniques of risk-reduction.

"Something I think is a good idea," I remarked abstractly, "would be for us to learn to have sex with friends. That would reduce the number of different partners and assure you knew who you were fucking with."

"Yeah," said Steve, his eyes following a strikingly handsome young blond man passing our table, "but for most of us that's sort of taboo."

"I know," I said, thinking about my relationship with Steve. I'd been attracted to him sexually when we first met, but sex had never happened and pretty soon that interest had faded. Now we were "sisters" (as they say). "But when you haven't got a sexual relationship going, it seems like the safest thing to do," I answered him.

"You're probably right," he said, still distracted by the blond.

Neither of us had been dating anybody for over a month. We were both a little lonely and a little horny. Earlier in the day we'd been consoling each other on the phone and had decided to take ourselves out for dinner and a drink. I was expecting to meet one of my roommates a little later across the street at the Stud.

Both Steve and I were in good health. We knew we didn't have amoebas or any of the exotic diseases going around. But you couldn't know about somebody you'd just met.

"That's why you have to be discriminating," we agreed.

We wandered over to the bar. I looked for my roommate but didn't see him. Well, our plans had been loose. Steve and I stood in the press of the crowd, enjoying the gay male energy around us. It was getting late, time to go home. I started to ask Steve if he wanted to accompany me on the bus for mutual safety, but was delaying to give him a chance to connect with somebody if he was going to.

Steve turned to me and said rather solemnly, "Would you like to take me home?" It wasn't addressed as an invitation to ride together on the bus, I knew. "Yes," I said simply, surprised and pleased. I kissed him on the mouth to seal the agreement and acknowledge that I understood his nuance.

We stopped by his house in the Castro for a minute, then walked over the 21st and Sanchez Hill to see the view of the city – a bejewelled goddess crouching cat-like on the hill sides.

Once at my apartment we showered together, sitting for awhile on the bottom of the tub under the warm running water, playfully imagining ourselves in a tropical rain forest, tentatively experimenting with touching one another's body, admiring the look of each other's chest and torso.

I'd seen his body before, of course. We'd changed clothes in front of one another. We'd gone to the gay beach at Land's End together. But, I realized, we'd never been together when we were in this wonderfully altered state of consciousness of sexual arousal. Now his body seemed different to me. Familiar, yes, but also newly alive, offering all sorts of new sensations: taste and smell and touch – things we'd hadn't shared before because we'd let the odd gay taboo against having sex with friends prevent us.

As I looked at Steve and touched his skin – feeling the texture of muscle in his shoulders, cupping his pecs in my hand, running my thumb in circles around his tits, allowing his slowly engorging cock to rest in my palm – I wondered why we'd ever taken that taboo seriously. What had it gotten us?

Before we returned to my room, out of modesty in case he ran into one of my roommates in the hall, Steve pulled back on the bright red jock strap he'd been wearing under his jeans, the kind with the narrow band. As I adjusted the lights back in the bedroom, got out the sexual paraphernalia, and selected soft late-night jazz on the radio, I noticed how sexy the jock strap looked on him. The red accentuated the healthy color of his skin. It looked erotic without seeming sleazy. Indeed, it looked playfully, sexily modest.

I laughed and walked over to him and cupped my hand around the webbing of the jock and kissed him primly on the lips. "How do you like the ensemble?" he said, joining me in the laugh.

We sat down cross-legged on the bed – me with my legs wrapped around Steve's torso so that our mouths could meet easily. We kissed affectionately. There was no romance, no impersonal hot passion, but there was deep love and caring, and excitement. We nuzzled together so that Steve's cock, now growing hard behind the confining web, pressed up against the base of my balls. I pulled myself up against his chest so that my cock was against his torso. I felt comfortable, pleased with Steve's body.

I slid away from him so I was kneeling opposite him. I bent forward and, pulling the strap down and out of the way, sucked him, liking (and feeling surprised at!) the size of his cock and his balls – thick and solid, full and generous. He then rose up on his knees, pulling me up with him, and slowly turned us so he could reach my cock with his mouth and we could sixty-nine. We licked each other's balls and burrowed with our tongues into the crease between the balls and thighs. The sensations made us both quiver.

We played with synchronizing our movements, watching the pressure build up inside our groins until we were about to shoot.

Abruptly we pulled back. Breathing hard, we turned and sat up again facing each other. I was sitting inside his half-crossed legs with my knees against his sides. Our relaxing cocks throbbed against each other as the intense pressure drained out of them. We smiled and laughed.

"Wow" one (or both) of us said. I slumped back against the pile of pillows behind me. I ran my gaze across his chest, enjoying the sight of him. And the closeness. I reached out and took him by the elbows. First I pulled myself up so I could reach his tits with my mouth. To make his chest easier for me to reach he leaned back, supporting himself with his arms behind him, and offered me each tit in turn to kiss and bite at. He moaned with pleasure.

Falling back into the pillows, I relaxed the straining muscles in the small of my back, then pulled him down against my chest. I felt his hard cock press against me, slipping easily into the crease alongside my balls. My own cock thrust straight up against his belly, rubbing against his taut, velvety skin just where the brush of fine black hair grew up toward his navel. His legs were still crossed underneath my buttocks. Supporting himself now on arms outstretched in front of him, his hands to either side of my shoulders, he straightened his legs, pushing up against me, lifting my butt and bending my knees. He pressed tightly against me, letting himself down onto me sprocket-fashion so that from our bellies up to our pecs more and more of our skin met with each thrust of our cocks.

We lay together, with him on top of me, our extended bodies pressing together. We held each other. We kissed tentatively. I pushed back on his shoulders so that he reared up. Pulling his mouth from mine, he looked directly in my eyes. His gaze was warm, friendly, trusting. There was no look of passionate romance or limerent expectation. We were friends. Long ago we'd passed the stage in our relationship when that kind of unconscious, compelling bond would have formed. But we weren't strangers to one another either. There was a sense of "conquest," but it came simply from seeing that we'd overcome the taboo about having sex with friends.

We talked a moment, speaking softly through sighs as we

caught our breath. We trusted each other, we agreed. We knew who each other was. After all, we'd known one another a couple of years. We'd watched each other go through affairs of the heart. We shared our spiritual lives with one another. We knew each other's health history. We'd known each other's lovers. We'd seen each other's lifestyle. We'd walked all over San Francisco comparing our expectations and dreams. I knew I didn't mind getting Steve's "karma" mixed up with mine. We had already done that. With sex with strangers you never know what kind of karma or fortune you're getting mixed up in. And I'm convinced that having sex with people commingles more than just body fluids. "That's why you have to be discriminating," Steve and I both recited simultaneously, accenting each word and smiling with each other as we acknowledged a theme of our earlier conversation.

"I think I've discriminated very nicely," I said, again admiring Steve's lean and muscled torso as he sat back on his knees between my legs. He positioned one of the pillows under the small of my back. "Me too," he giggled rather solemnly.

"Can I get rid of this?" I asked and started to pull on the elastic strap that had gotten pushed down and was binding around his scrotum.

"Don't you like the color?" he feigned a look of hurt pride. Then added, "Yeah, I think it's time." He rolled away from me so he could pull the jock strap off. His movement allowed me to reach the pump bottle on the table by the bed. As he repositioned himself, sitting astride my legs, I squirted some lubricant into my hand and greased up both our balls and our cocks. They quickly tightened up again.

I closed both my hands around us, holding our cocks tight against one another, sliding my hands up and down in that ancient gesture of manhood.

Steve straightened out and came down so he was lying on top of me again. With our cocks hard we thrust rhythmically against each other's belly. After a while, Steve pulled back and slipped his cock under my balls and between my legs. I locked my feet around one another to increase the pressure holding his cock between my thighs.

As he rode me, I could feel the head of his cock grazing my asshole. I struggled to straighten my spine and tuck my ass up so that he slid more easily against me. I relaxed my abdomen and felt myself opening up to him. He wasn't fucking me, but my ass was alive with every thrust. I met each downward thrust of his with my own upward thrust so that my cock slid along his belly and his cock slid between my legs and against the electric nerve center of my asshole.

I came close to coming. Then, pulling back, I rolled us over on our sides. The change in position helped me hold off. We still kept up the rhythmic thrusting. I knew I couldn't put off coming through many more cycles. I pulled my face back so I could look him in the eyes. He returned my look and with an elfish twinkle. We exchanged an unspoken signal. And, holding each other's gaze, increased the rhythm and the force of our thrusts against each other.

I slipped into the pattern of breathing and deep thrusting that slowly, and then more quickly, triggered my orgasm. Deep inside I could feel the pressure rising, building, and then suddenly rushing upward. I arched my back and groaned uncontrollably as the waves of tension and release, tension and release shot through me. In that odd state of detachment and self-observation that often accompanies orgasm, I marveled at the fact that this man who'd brought me so much pleasure was a friend of mine, a man I delighted to be with in so many ways. And now we'd found a new way to be together

The waves of pleasure flowed smoothly right into Steve. He looked at me. His eyes widened. He looked almost surprised as his body kicked against my hips and thighs. A long deep moan accompanied the shots from his cock.

I delayed separating. My cock felt long, soft and smooth, and electric against his belly. We continued to thrust lightly as the aftershocks rippled through us. Then, gulping for breath and laughing, we hugged tight.

The sex had been marvelous. And it had been safe. No exchange of fluids. And no less ecstatic on that account. I was pleased to see we'd followed the risk-reduction advice without even having to think about it. How good to be with a man I didn't have to worry I'd turn off by considering such timely things. We held one another while our pulses and breathing settled down. I kissed his neck and shoulder and he nibbled my ear as we cuddled together. We pulled the covers over us to keep out the cold of the San Francisco night.

Soon we got up, pee'd, and showered again. His body felt wonderfully warm against mine as we fell asleep a little later. Nice to have a friend.

The next morning, by the way, Steve left me the red jock strap as a souvenir of that first sex together. And that wasn't the last time we enjoyed this new dimension of our relationship. And we're still friends. I wear the jock sometimes and I remind myself I don't have to be constricted by the wrong taboos.

No One Gets Hurt

GEORGE WHITMORE

"We know you're in there, Reilly! Come out with your hands up and no one gets hurt!"

It sounded like the door was coming off its hinges. I groaned and turned over in bed.

"Aw, come on, Reilly." He was coaxing me now, lips close to the keyhole. "Come on out and play."

It was gutless of me just to lie there, head burrowed under the pillow, and let him carry on that way. I should have answered the door at the first rap. But now it was too late. I decided he could hardly kick up more of a fuss than he already had. I was out, o-u-t, out.

"I have a present for you. Don't you want to see what I have? Something you've always wanted."

I snorted – quietly, into the pillow.

"Something very, very nice."

He had to leave eventually.

And eventually, after more wheedling, foot shuffling and grumbling, he did.

It was Ralph. Ralph who used to be one of my friends – sort of – before.

Before we buried Eddie, before Eddie got it, before.

When we buried Eddie, I went into my apartment and didn't

come out. Well . . . that's an overstatement. I went to work. When I came home in the evenings, I had a few belts, sometimes ate dinner, took a few pills and turned in. This went on for quite a while — six, seven months?

I knew Eddie since we were in junior high together. We moved to the city together. We'd even lived together at one point. There were some wonderful times with Eddie, but I couldn't remember them now. It hurt too much. What I remembered when I closed my eyes was Eddie in the hospital at the end. He wasn't Eddie at the end.

Why Eddie? What did Eddie ever do? Why not me?

"You've got to keep on living," Ralph said.

"Yeah? How?"

It wasn't just Eddie. It was a whole chunk of my life in the garbage. Unlike Eddie, I'd been a pig — I don't know how else to put it — most of my adult life. Some people arrange their lives around food or work or growing African violets, like my mother. I arranged my life around sex. Three, four, sometimes five nights a week. And I loved it.

You can laugh if you want — I loved the anonymity of it. For every tired old face (like mine) in every sewer I dropped into, there was always a fresh one. Where'd they keep coming from? Jersey? But then, who was asking questions?

That all ended when Eddie did.

"What you're having," Ralph said over the phone one day, "is a phobic reaction."

"Keep your phobics to yourself."

"No — you are. And no, I won't."

"Everything's changed, kiddo," I said, trying to sound flip. "Everything. Nothing's the same."

"Reilly, this is just the other side of the coin."

"What do you mean?"

"With you it's always extremes."

"Yeah?"

"Now you're mad at me."

"No I'm not. I'm interested in hearing what you have to say — based on your extensive knowledge of my psyche."

"Well, if you're really interested . . . "

But then I hung up on him.

I'd had enough of Ralph's cut-rate psychoanalysis – his blather about "the mourning process" – his "do you want to talk about it?" – up to here.

I have to hand it to Ralph, he stuck it out longer than most of my friends, most of whom I wasn't speaking to anymore anyway because: where were they when Eddie was in the hospital?

I told a few of them just what I thought of them in a few well chosen words. So the dinner invitations and the spur of the moment calls to go out dancing dwindled down to nothing. I even got fewer Christmas's cards than usual that year. And it was all right with me. No one who hadn't seen Eddie in his hospital bed, who hadn't seen Eddie disappear by degrees and get replaced by a gaunt stranger the way I had could understand anyway.

Yeah – my hot, hip friends. Most of those guys I'd danced with in one club or the other for years. Some of them, I'd held their pricks while they peed on some dude in the tub at the Mineshaft. Others, I'd held their heads while they puked on the sidewalk from Osterizing their drugs. I'd laughed and kidded and even had some pretty heavy conversations with them early in the morning as the bar was closing over the years. They were fixtures in my life. They were fixtures all right. As far as I knew, they were still keeping the bar at the Spike from falling down.

But Ralph, who I had nothing in common with whatsoever, nothing but Eddie – Ralph was harder to shake.

"Look," I apologized one night after I just bit off his head, "I'm sorry – I know you mean well. Just let me work it out."

"No," he said quietly at the other end of the line. "I'm sorry. Maybe I have a few things to work out myself. We both loved Eddie."

"Yeah," I said. It caught in my throat. "I'm going to hang up now."

I wasn't able to cry.

Ralph was Eddie's special friend. But they were so unalike, it was hard to figure. At first I thought it must have been sex, but it wasn't. Old Eddie was a romantic. If I was looking for nothing but sex all those years, Eddie was looking for love, of that I'm now sure. At first I thought it was sex – why else would Eddie hang out with a decorator? But "I like his sense of humor," Eddie told me. This was puzzling. I'd never noticed Ralph had any to speak of.

He was one of those nose-to-the-grindstone types. And spending hours flipping through little books of fabric samples or picking out the right doorknob for Mrs. Vanwhatsis's boudoire you'd think would take a sense of humor, but Ralphie was very serious about his business. Downright defensive, I thought.

"What'd I say?"

Eddie wrinkled up his nose. "Pud. No wonder he walked out."

"No, what'd I say? I just said it was a good thing he put it on the couch because if you wore it you'd get arrested."

"He's doing my whole apartment for nothing."

"He's a sucker then."

"It's in his nature. He's a giving person."

There was a kind of prissiness in Eddie's voice when he said that, like Ralph was Mother Theresa.

I couldn't fathom it. I couldn't fathom their chummy thing. What'd they talk about? Eddie was no dumb-bell but he wasn't any Einstein. What he was was a bricklayer.

Ralph, on the other hand, had pretensions. Not only was his apartment fit for a queen, he read *New York* magazine relentlessly, so as to keep up on the latest buzz-words. He went to church "for the music." He wore colored socks.

When Eddie's mother, the old bitch, came to see her son buried after not talking to him since she kicked him out at sixteen, Ralph took care of her. He kept her away from me, for starters.

For that I was grateful. "It's just too bad you couldn't keep her from going to the cemetery."

That was some scene. Me, Ralph and Eddie's family – the hypocritical old bag tried to crawl into the open grave.

"She feels guilty," Ralph said, sitting back in the cab.

"Guilt's easy."

"You're right. I don't think she ever loved him."

"Fucking old . . ."

"Easy. I feel guilty too."

"You?"

He'd been up to the hospital almost as often as I had.

"Yeah. How can you not?"

"Well I don't."

He didn't say anything to that. Only later, he brought up "survivor guilt" – and I hung up on him that night, too.

But he hung in there. He always wanted to get together for coffee or a drink. He always made a point of it to "check in" twice a week. I thought it was his way of hanging onto Eddie.

Life will out. One spring day I started thinking about dick again. Dick, dick, dick. It crept into my dreams – me, who hadn't been able to wrap his hand around even his own for months. Dick. I saw them, big ones, drooling in front of my face. Shaving, I looked at my face in the mirror. Flushed from my shower, it was pink, like a dick.

Life will out. You can't hold it down. I was all right at work – I'd maintained a strict line for years – but not so all right on the street. Dicks and asses. I started looking again.

I'd come home and flop down on the bed, unzip and take it out – but nothing.

So I figured, Perfect. This is worse than not being interested in the first place.

"Why don't you go to the New York Jacks?"

"Come on, Ralph. Sex by the rule-book? A bunch of guys standing around feeling each other up?"

"What'd you do in the Mineshaft?"

"We didn't fill out dance cards."

"Just a suggestion."

"I tell you what, Ralphie. When you join, you can bring me in as a member."

He was still calling. When I didn't answer for a couple of days, sometimes he'd drop by – the lock on the outside door to the slum I called home was last operable in 1885, when the building opened.

And that's what he was doing outside my door that night. Trying to get me to come out for a cappucino (the guy couldn't just have an ordinary cup of coffee like everyone else) or a movie (some jerky German art film) or open up the door so we could have one of our little chats. Any other door in the leather flats I called home he could have knocked on and made somebody's day. He was hunky, there's no denying. Too bad he was such a nerd.

"Reilly! Come on, Reilly! I heard you moving around. I saw the light."

I stood in front of the refrigerator, holding the door open. Damn, I thought. I should go out and punch him in the mouth. He'd been lurking outside the door – how long? Jesus. He must have been down on his hands and knees to see the light come on from the refrigerator. Jesus. It was one in the morning. All I wanted was another beer.

It was getting sick. Obsessive. Old Ralph was going round the bend.

"Come on out, Reilly. Come out for a drink. I know you were at the Spike last weekend, Reilly. Come out for a drink with me."

In spite of myself, I said, "How'd you know that?"

"I have spies, Reilly. Let's go out for a drink. I'll even go to the Spike with you." When I didn't answer, he said, "I'm even dressed for it."

I popped open a beer.

"You should see me, Reilly."

I walked across the room and sat on the bed. Somehow, with Ralph right outside the door, my little studio seemed even smaller, vulnerable to attack. I realized, I was afraid of him. He was nuts.

I imagined him in – what? Leather? No way. A jean jacket? I shuddered thinking what his version of what to wear to the Spike was. I could already smell his cologne through the door.

Yes, I'd been to the Spike the weekend before – in and out. Also to the Ramrod and the Anvil. But I went home after a beer in each. It hurt too much, seeing what I wanted and knowing I couldn't have it.

"I know it's late, Reilly, but it's Friday night, for Christsake. Let's get down."

That made me choke on my beer.

"Boogie," he added.

"You're nuts, Ralph."

"Let me be your Virgil, Reilly."

"My what?"

"Let me guide you through the underworld."

"Get lost."

"I know what you need, Reilly."

I put my feet up on the TV. "You do, do you?"

"Yeah." He was mumbling against the door. "I know just what you need."

I didn't answer.

"You," he almost whispered, "need to get laid."

That made me mad.

"Dick, Reilly."

"Fuck you."

"Oh, hit a nerve? There are ways to do it, Reilly. Ways you've never imagined, not in your wildest . . ."

"Just fuck off, Ralph, or I'll call the cops!" Suddenly, I was shouting, and God help me, I was up on my feet now, holding the can up. I would have thrown it against the door. I realized I was shaking.

He heard me all right. It must have scared him because after a while I heard him shuffle across the landing and then walk slowly down the stairs. I counted the flights. I heard the broken front door swing to with a clatter.

I sat down. The guy was a nut. I've often noticed, the ones who think they have your number, the Florence Nightingale types – they're more fucked up than anyone.

It was, as they say, as big as a baby's arm. I could feel it. He wouldn't give it to me, just kept rubbing it over my face, poking it into my eyes, running it across my lips. Pretty soon I knew it like the back of my hand, each ridge, each vein, every wrinkle – in the dark.

"Keep the mouth closed, faggot. Zip it up. That's a good boy."

The ropes were beginning to hurt. Every once in a while he'd pull me up by the hair, slap me, then slap me across the face with the dick. It made a soft sound. It stung like hell.

Heel on the floor – I think, I couldn't see – he held down my dick with his boot, applied steady pressure, ground it against the planks. Strangely, it only hurt at the head. It felt like the head was going to bust.

"Shut up, faggot. Stop whining. I hate a whiner, God I hate a whiner. Why'd they give me a pussy?" He ground down on my dick. "Pussies. They always give me pussies."

I made a little sound in my throat. Couldn't help it.

He kicked me in the gut – not hard, but enough to take my breath away.

"Keep the mouth closed."

Then the dick again, over my face.

How long? Hours? He was good. He kept me like that, panting, on the edge, sweating it out, for hours. After hours of it, I began to beg, then he started slapping me with his open hand, on one side of the head, then the other. Once I started begging, though, I couldn't stop. He didn't say anything. He grunted, almost inaudibly, every time he slapped me. I was babbling, slobbering, sobbing. I loved it.

"Jesus." I fell out of bed. "Another night like that, I'll be ready for Bellevue."

But I looked at my belly, glistening in the weak light from the window. It was six in the morning. I must have cum three or four times during the night.

"That wasn't a wet dream, it was a double feature."

Fifty-third and Fifth. That's where your whole life passes before your eyes. I don't know what it is. Maybe it's the stores. Maybe it's the museum. Maybe it's just rotten karma. But somehow you see everyone you ever knew sooner or later at Fifty-third and Fifth.

After the night I threatened to call the cops, I didn't see Ralph for, it must have been months, then I saw him at Fifty-third and Fifth. It was summer. He was in his decorator drag – Italian suit, flashy silk tie, handkerchief dripping out of his breast pocket – and carrying a big leather portfolio.

"Reilly! How you doing?"

"I'm on my lunch hour."

"Great. Let's have lunch."

"I mean, I just ate."

"Oh. How's it going?"

"Okay."

He literally had me up against a wall. I would have had to step on his blue suede shoes to get away.

"I've missed you," he said.

"Yeah?"

"Of course. You must have thought I was some kind of lunatic – the last time we, uh, talked."

"Matter of fact . . . "

"Yeah, well, sorry."

"That's all right." I found it hard to look into his wet brown eyes. They reminded me of a nice little puppy dog's.

"Listen," he said, "I was thinking – you have a birthday coming up, don't you?"

This irritated me – that he would remember. I thought he must have a little book with birthdays in it. That irritated me even more.

"So can I take you out to dinner or something?"

"I – well, I'm not going to be in town."

"Oh." He didn't believe me, of course, and he was right, but he swallowed and swallowed the lie. "Too bad. Well maybe some other time."

"Yeah." I didn't move away but stood against the wall, immobile now, and somehow more indifferent than when I was shifting around.

"Okay," he said, looking away down the street, then up at the sky, then down at his feet. "See you around then."

"Great," I said.

And he walked away.

You know, I'd expected him to say something like "Eddie would have wanted us to keep being friends" but he never did.

I was not out of town on my birthday. It was a Saturday night and I was at home. Friday night I'd made the rounds of the bars and actually picked up someone, went back to his house with him after an hour of negotiations about as exciting as filling out your taxes, took off my clothes, and – nothing.

He was hot, too.

"Mind if I?"

"Be my guest," I said.

He jacked off into a rubber then went into the bathroom and flushed it down the toilet.

It was Saturday night. I'd actually bought myself a cupcake, though I didn't go so far as to put one of those little candles on it or sing myself a song. Let's just say I was feeling sorry for myself, alone on my birthday, unable not to think about Eddie and the birthday parties Eddie gave me over the years . . .

Close. We were close. He knew everything about me – that I liked canneloni or manicotti but never knew which to ask for in a restuarant because I could never remember which was which, that I still kept my Tenderfoot badge in the top bureau drawer because I was so proud I got that far, that Susan Ginsberg broke my heart in 8th grade. What I was and what I thought, what I once wanted to be, exactly what I liked to do in bed – everything. He took everything with him.

I left the cupcake half-eaten and was just pouring myself a drink, about to toast Eddie, when it began.

BANG BANG BANG BANG-BANG.

Someone was pounding on the door.

"Open up, Reilly! We know you're in there!"

But it wasn't Ralph.

"Come on, Reilly! Open the fucking door or we'll bash it in!"

Two of them. Big butch nasty voices. A chill ran across my bare back. I thought, irrationally, the cops. I moved toward the door, then hesitated. What if they're . . . How would muggers get my name? It wasn't on the mailbox. Who the fuck were they? If they were the cops . . . But they'd say they were the cops. And why the fuck would the cops come banging on my door?

BANG BANG BANG BANG-BANG.

Then: "It's nothin' lady. Just a little private business between Mr. Reilly and us. Go back inside."

Jesus, the neighbors must think I'm dealing drugs.

"Come on, Reilly. You want us to bash the door in or what? Open the door, Reilly."

Quieter this time, but I stood trembling in the middle of the floor, naked in only my jockey shorts.

"Make it easy on yourself, Reilly."

"Who – who are you?"

"Open the door and find out."

"Go away or I'll – call the cops." My voice shook. It didn't even convince me.

"Open up, Reilly."

I moved toward the door.

"What do you want?"

"You, Reilly."

"Open up, Reilly," the other said. "Or I'm going to kick it in."

I hesitated again, just a second, then there was an ear- splitting crash and the door flew open.

Big and butch they were. And dressed in leather from the tips of their boots to the tops of their heads – leather masks. They were huge, hulks, but fast.

Clink-clink.

Handcuffs.

I was kicking and even trying to bite. One of them sat on me on the floor while the other one closed the door.

"Relax, Reilly, and you won't get hurt." He bounced up and down on me a few times.

"Relax, Reilly," the other one said, tucking my feet into his armpits.

"Why hurt yourself," the first one said.

"Yeah. Why hurt yourself?"

I was putting up a pretty good fight. They were both sweating.

Soon I stopped struggling, though. It became a choice between struggling and breathing.

"That's better."

"Yeah, Reilly, much better."

"Now, let's put on your jeans, Reilly."

"Gonna be a good boy?"

"Don't kick, now, Reilly."

"Ready?"

I let myself be dressed. Not much choice. The bigger one of the two was still sitting on my chest with his big basket bumping against my chin.

"Now, Reilly, time to go. Stand up, baby. Time to go see Killer."

"Killer? Who's that?" I didn't like the sound of my voice. It was high-pitched. "This is some kind of mistake or something. I don't know any Killer."

"Yes you do, Reilly." He yanked me to my feet. "And he's waiting."

"Must not keep Killer waiting, Reilly."

Barefoot, shirtless — they dragged me down the stairs and out onto the street, pushed me into a van. The doors clanged shut behind me. Even in the summer heat, the steel floor of the van was cold.

A guy could get hurt, I thought. Yet they hadn't hurt me — yet. They were careful not to hurt me. This almost scared me more.

The regulation cuffs bit into my wrists.

The smaller (ha! smaller) one revved up the engine. The bigger (not much) one wedged himself between the bucket seats, kneeled over me on the floor and blindfolded me. I just had time to wonder what color the hankie was.

It was a wild ride, endless, and I slithered and slid across the floor of the van like a sack of shit.

"Hey! Watch it! Jesus, you guys are going to kill me!"

"Lay flat, Reilly. Center of gravity, babe. Don't hurt yourself."

"Yeah," the other one snickered. "Don't hurt yourself."

"Killer don't like bruises, Reilly. He don't mind givin' 'em, but he don't like damaged goods."

"Don't like bruised fruit."

"Yeah, bruised fruit."

They thought this was comic.

Endless. There aren't many cobblestone streets left in Manhattan, but we crossed every one of them that night — and hit bottom in every legendary pothole the city has. I moaned.

"Oh, didum bite his tongue?" they baby-talked to me.

"Keep down on the floor, fucker!"

By the time they brought the van to a jarring halt, I was scared shitless. Snot was running out of my nose. My mind was going ninety miles a minute. That they were going to kill me was running neck and neck with the possibility that they were going to dump me in the middle of Times Square. But they weren't asking me which one I'd prefer.

It was somewhere between the two. They hauled me out of the back of the van, set me down on the sidewalk and yanked the blindfold off.

We were in front of the Spike.

"Go inside," the big one rasped into my ear. "Into the bar. Do not pass go, do not collect one hundred dollars, fuckface, go into the bar. Killer's waiting."

"We'll be right behind you."

They gave me a shove, then another.

So in I went, hands cuffed behind my back. All I could think was how I was going to scream my head off when I got through the door.

The place was packed. It was like old-home week. I stood inside the door, still shaking, still tasting snot. But I didn't scream. I opened my mouth, then closed it. The ludicrousness of it hit me. It hit me, this was a colossal practical joke of some kind – so what if my wrists were raw and I had floor-burns across my shoulders. Who kidnaps you and takes you to the Spike? Sick faggots, that's who.

And the familiar faces at the bar – people I hated, people I kind of liked, people I felt totally nothing about – were grinning at me, some of them at least, the ones who were even looking at me. No one said anything, though.

I was too cool to start asking who the fuck was behind this.

Instead, I walked up to the bar, shouldered in between two queens, leaned against it facing the room and waited.

And waited. Pretty soon, I started shivering. I was right in the path of the air-conditioning. And sooner or later, when everyone had stopped looking at me, I started feeling stupid. That's when I saw him.

And at that exact moment, the bartender snapped a dog collar around my neck and tossed the leash at him.

"Come on, fuckface! March!"

He wouldn't give it to me, just kept rubbing it over my face, poking it into my eyes, running it across my lips. Pretty soon I knew it like the back of my hand, each ridge, each vein, every wrinkle – in the dark.

"Keep the mouth closed, faggot. Zip it up. That's a good boy."

The ropes were beginning to hurt. Every once in a while he'd pull me up by the hair, slap me, then slap me across the face with the dick. It made a soft sound. It stung like hell.

He meant business. I'd only made him laugh once, in the van – that is, he didn't laugh, he just turned away, but not before I saw the smile creeping across his face.

But now he meant business. He was really into it. Just before he shoved me through the door and sent me sprawling across the floor, he slapped me smartly across the face and wiped the grin off it. Leaning close to me so I could smell his rotten cigar breath, he whispered low and mean.

"Just behave yourself, faggot."

"Right."

Another slap.

"Sir, yes, sir!" I was trembling with excitement. I couldn't help it. 'You gonna fuck me, sir?" I couldn't keep the insolence out of my voice, though I tried to because, goddam if he wasn't getting me hot.

"Fucking's too good for you, faggot. Just behave yourself, pussy."

"Sir, yes, sir!"

"And no one gets hurt."

The New Cosmic Consciousness

TRIPP VANDERFORD

Exercise – at least to certain individuals – is only *one* reason for going to a gym. While serious body builders may devote hours each day to a rigorous weight lifting regime, social intercourse is an integral part of each and every workout. The gym, no doubt, is a place to meet with friends, compare notes and gossip . . . see and be seen.

My friend, Pete, and I were doing all of the above while we pumped our pecs to oblivion.

Pete had prostrated himself to the bench press. His gray T-shirt, stained black with sweat, glued him to the leather throne. Fist-size mounds of pectoral flesh swelled from heaving chest. His clean-shaven chin dimpled as Pete clenched the bar and strained to lift it from its rack.

Like a faithful guard, I stood behind him. Should Pete's strength falter beneath those incredible weights, it was my duty to guide the bar back onto its cradle. Considering myself capable of attending to more than one task at a time, I did this while keeping an eye peeled to the new gym member who graced our presence.

"Jesus, be sweet!" I uttered a three-word prayer. "Would you take a look at what walked in?"

Pete hoisted the weights above his chest and scowled, "Give me a break!" Crescents of green peeked through squinted eyes. "I'm pressing two-fifty, for Christsakes!"

Completing his set, my body building buddy slid off the bench and combed a confident hand through his mane of dark, damp ringlets. "Where is he?" Pete's tone implied little enthusiasm.

"Over there." With great discretion, I nodded my head. "By the mirror."

"Which mirror?" A symphony of sarcasm rang from Pete's voice. "This entire gym is paneled with mirrors."

"The mirror in front of the *dumbbell* rack," I gritted orthodontically straightened teeth. "You can't *miss* seeing him."

Pete craned his neck. What he saw triggered a smile on his lips and a bulge in his gym shorts.

The subject of our attention was tall, fair and handsome in a classic sort of way. Form-fitting T-shirt and faded red shorts did little to mask a body that was a study in symmetrical design. Sun-streaked hair was cut in a conservative style and parted to one side. Two large aquamarine pools shimmered above model-material cheeks. Finer, more perfect features could not have been chiseled by the hands of Michelangelo himself.

As the phenomenal youth returned an awesome-size weight to its station, cool, sleepy eyes detected our stares. The self-appointed god wore a vapid expression, one which suggested neither interest nor acknowledgement of interest.

Pete furrowed his brow. "The attitude I can take," he sighed. "It's the indifference I can't handle."

I ignored the comment. My imagination ran rampant as I mentally undressed my flesh and muscle fantasy. "I wonder if he wears white jockey shorts?"

"Judging from the *obscene* protrusion that's straining against his pant leg," Pete snorted, "I'd guess he's not wearing anything except what meets the eye."

"That ass!" I drooled. "What I wouldn't do just to spread those cheeks and lick his slit!"

"You're disgusting!" Pete screwed his aquiline nose in a way that reminded me of a peacock who may have had his last tail feather plucked. "Have you forgotten that there's a certain fatal illness that tends to travel along the circles in which we run? *That* doesn't sound like a very safe thing to do."

"I'm perfectly well-informed," My tone became smug, "but it doesn't hurt to dream."

"Dream all you'd like." My friend's lips curled into a pessimistic frown. "That guy's only concern is himself. I can spot his kind in a minute."

"Enough talk." I shrugged my shoulders and lowered myself on the bench press. "Let's get going with this workout."

Eight, nine, ten times I cleared the bar above my chest. Exercise completed, the pleasurable pain of exhausted muscle tissue shot across my chest, electrified my body and charged my most private muscle. A virile vision of red and blond and muscle flashed before me. I began to feel dizzy, light-headed and weak at the knees.

"Think that'll be it for me today," I said with a tremble.

"What!" Pete shrieked. "We haven't done our arms yet!"

"That guy," I spoke in *sotte voce,* "he's heading for the shower."

"Oh?" My friend arched a suspicious brow.

"The opportunity of a lifetime to check out the merchandise."

"Go for it, big fella." Sarcasm desecrated Pete's blessing. "If love doesn't slap you in the face, I will."

An appropriate groan accompanied a fond farewell. Threading my way through a maze of Nautilus machines and tons of iron weights, I charted a trail to the lockers. There, I spotted him.

He was posing for the mirror, flexing his monumental tits and wearing nothing more than a confident grin . . . and a pair of clean, white briefs.

My stomach somersaulted – twice. I clenched my jaw to mask the lusty yearning that I harbored for the stud. *"Fawning is* NOT *becoming to a twenty-eight year old man,"* I reminded myself.

While pretending to dial my combination lock, I stole a sideways glance to my right. The hunk was strutting toward his locker, opening its door, and to my horror, stepping into a pair of Levis.

"Damn!" I kicked the locker, kicked it hard.

"Clear the combination and try it again," a baritone instructed. "Kicking's the hard way to get it open."

The voice jolted me back to earth. "Pardon?"

"I said to try clearing the combination."

"Yeah . . . right," I sputtered.

Mister Look-so-Good buttoned a wrinkled oxford shirt, then tossed his gym bag over one Herculean shoulder. "I'm Reid," he announced as I stripped off my sweaty gym gear.

Nodding my head in Joe Cool fashion, I extended a bone-crushing handshake, "Tripp."

Liquid eyes collided with mine, skirted my torso and lingered for one fraction of a second on my lower extremity. "Nice to meet you." His focus returned to eye level.

I draped my nakedness with a towel. "Same here," a steady voice camouflaged my unimaginable excitement.

"Take it easy, big guy," Reid mimicked my Joe Cool nod as he turned to leave.

"Be still my heart," I told myself. *"He was ONLY being friendly. He probably has a lover . . . or a disposition towards Italians or redheads or some other exotic type. Maybe he's straight . . . or at least THINKS he is. My luck he's carrying some lethal virus and would pass it along to me if we DID fuck."* Bracing myself for ultimate rejection, I ambled toward the showers.

The large communal stall could as well have been an exhibition hall. Four-star hunks crowded elbow to asshole as they soaped and showered, modeled and displayed their sculpted bodies.

I was no exception. With great deliberateness, I lathered my primely pumped pecs, my muscle-riveted abdomen, my Pride and Joy. Five years, five *faithful* years I had invested in pumping iron. My body witnessed such great devotion to this most narcissistic of sports – and I was more than happy to display the trophy it had earned.

Icy daggers pelted my shoulders as I turned to rinse my back. Across from me, a strapping moustache made little effort to disguise his penchant for sightseeing. His stare was fixed to my jewels; his excitement quite apparent.

Flattered, yet unaroused, I ignored his admiration and parted from his view. While my admirer was both handsome and hung, a solitary obsession monopolized my thoughts: Reid.

Towel in hand, I stationed myself before omnipresent mirrors. The reflection bolstered my ego. I *liked* the way I imagined myself to look to other people: handsomely featured, magnificently muscular and confident beyond a doubt.

A bitter smile played about my lips. I was in the prime of life, had worked hard to get there – and was shadowed by a perilous age that haunted me and others of my kind.

"You look like a stud," a familiar voice blended praise with causticity. "And your dallywhacker's the talk of the gym. Now get over yourself."

I rolled my eyes in a way that was not particularly in keeping with the image I like to project. "Lot of good it does me," my bitterness lashed out at Pete.

"No score with Boy Wonder?" Peter understood my disappointment, offered a sympathetic smile.

"His name's Reid. He *does* wear white jockey shorts. And he did *not* take a shower."

"Sounds like primo pig!"

"He actually seemed rather nice." I draped the towel across my shoulders and flexed for the mirror. "We introduced ourselves in the locker room."

"At least he *spoke* to you." Pete hooked his towel on a wooden peg. "That's a start."

I gave my friend a Big-Fuck'n-Deal look. "Always the bridesmaid, never the bride."

"It's your own fault," Pete called over his shoulder as he sauntered toward the stall.

Whether by coincidence or by fate, our paths crossed again and again. Night after night, I saw Reid at the gym. His nods and smiles were tinged with calculated nonchalance and titillated me beyond all reason. Still, he rarely spoke to me; gave no signal of more than a passing interest.

This only spurred my passion. The more unobtainable he appeared, the more I desired him. I wanted the manboy, wanted him *fiercely*.

As I curled a barbell close against my heart, I spotted Reid from peripheral vision. He was studying his reflection in mirrored walls, absorbed with himself and oblivious to my admiring glances. His obsession with physical beauty rivaled even my own.

"Hi Dog-Face," Pete greeted me in his familiar manner. Dressed in khakis and polo shirt, my friend was hardly outfitted for weight lifting.

I pumped my biceps a final time, then cradled the weight onto its rack. "What's this wearing Prep School Drag to the gym?" I scoffed.

"No workout for me tonight." Guilt dripped from apologetic eyes. "There's a Bette Davis revival showing uptown this evening. Wanna come?"

I looked at Pete as though he had lost his noodle. "I have more important things to do . . . like pumping my tits. Besides, I could care *less* about Bette Davis *or* her films.

"How dare you blaspheme the Diva of Drama!" Pete spoke with indignation. "And you call yourself gay!"

Ignoring this verbal slap-in-the-face, I turned the other cheek. As just reward for my martyrdom, I chanced to find Reid looking toward me.

"I think you're only a homosexual because of the sex," Pete accused. "All you think about is dick, dick, dick!"

"Pete," my affected smile foreshadowed a brilliant rebuttal. "Who amongst us holds a charter membership to every jerk-off club in the city? And who owns a *complete* collection of every *Blueboy* magazine since the date of its conception? And *who* had a date Saturday night that lasted 'til Sunday afternoon? And which of us has not gotten laid in more than a month?"

My message was quite clear. Pete offered a surly smile as he scanned the wall-to-wall assembly of beefcake beauties. "Don't let you-know-who distract your workout."

"Bye, Pete." I noticed Reid striding toward me, and encouraged Pete to leave to see his stupid movie.

"Maybe I *will* skip Bette and hang around here for a while," Pete tested our friendship.

"*Bye*, Pete," I repeated through clenched teeth.

Pete took the cue. No sooner had my friend made his exit,

than Reid appeared by my side. I could tell by the superstud's expression that he wanted *something* – and I was willing to give him what*ever* that was.

"Mind lending a hand at the lateral bar?" Reid wasted no words on social amenities.

"Sure." A veil of apathy cloaked my eagerness.

I followed him across the room. As though calculating an algebraic equation, Reid studied the stack of iron plates which rested at the foot of a scaffold-like frame. Pegging a pin in the heaviest of weights, he gripped the horizontal bar which joined the pulley that was rigged to the plates.

"When I get in position," Reid instructed, "wrap your legs around my waist and hold me down."

My head swam at the thought, yet I remained the forever Joe Cool.

Reid curled square hands around the bar. A stack of iron plates rose to scaffold's summit as he lowered his small, round buns to the floor.

Seated behind him, I clasped my legs around his middle. My arms embraced his remarkable chest. And I trembled ever so slightly.

Straining, grunting, threatening to burst a gut, Reid commanded the bar behind his neck four, five, six times. Streams of perspiration trickled down his neck, soaked his plain white T-shirt. Veins, thick purple cords, swelled from tortured arms. His hardboiled lateral muscles ballooned with each repetition.

The smell of masculine sweat, the touch of his hard and heaving body, caused my temples, among other things, to throb. A hard ache thrashed in my gym shorts. And I could *feel* my manhood pressing against Reid's back.

More quickly that I would have favored, he finished the exercise. Unshackled from the bar, and looming before me, Reid studied my obvious need. "Have a problem?" Amusement tinted his coy remark.

"Yeah," I said without apology. "Wanna do something about it?"

"Maybe." Reid guarded his reply with a crooked, Joe Cool smile.

"Meet me outside the gym in half an hour." My peter-powered passion prohibited further subtlety. "Then we can take a walk back to my place . . . if you'd like."

Reid hesitated, chewed on a nail. "How about meeting across the street . . . at The Malt 'n' Whey Cafe? I could go for something to drink."

"A deal," I nodded to agree.

A train of thoughts trailed me across the Nautilus circuit as I continued my regime. *"An actual DATE . . . We'll linger over a malt . . . Violins will play in the background . . . We'll stare lovingly in each others' eyes . . . He'll whisper sweet nothings from across our table . . . It'll be just like in the movies!"* My face contorted with pain as I heaved the bar above my shoulders. *"Then I'll invite him back to my apartment . . . And tear off his little white jockey shorts!"*

This is what I imagined would happen. Unfortunately, things did not turn out exactly that way.

Leg lifts, arm curls, shoulder shrugs completed, we rendezvoused amidst a proliferation of potted ferns. Our waitress, a young woman who looked as though she may have been the daughter of Mother Earth, placed a Papaya Protein Malt on Reid's side of the table; on mine, a Frozen Fruit Frappe. A loud, protesting song, a record I seem to recall my older brother purchasing circa 1968, blared from the jukebox.

Reid sealed his lips to a straw and inhaled the pinkish-orange concoction with a single slurp. "Pumping iron sure can work up your thirst." A sheepish grin substituted for etiquette.

Already, I suspected that the evening may not be as romantic as the one I had envisioned. Sipping from my citrus swill, I manufactured a smile which would have come naturally to Emily Post, "Nothing like a protein pecker-upper after a hard workout!"

Reid's impish chortle implied an appreciation for innuendo.

"Care for a nightcap at my place?" I winked one bedroom-eye. "I could whip up something fresh and creamy."

From the look on the Golden God's face, it seemed as if I had invited him to slide down a razor blade – and into a pool of alcohol. A papaya-pink upper lip stiffened. Hands clenched into white-knuckled fists. Reid furrowed his brow and scanned the room as though to search for some invisible enemy that lurked behind potted ferns. Beneath our table, an anxious foot tapped Morse.

The signals were not clear, yet I recognized distress. Reid, gym hero, superstud and star, had reverted to a nervous adolescent. Unable to speak, eyes glazed with alarm, this hardly seemed like the confident thoroughbred I had met at the gym.

"Did I push your panic button?" I joked to ease the spiraling tension that hovered between us.

"No, nothing like that," Reid attempted to sound confident. His posture, however, stated the opposite. "It's just that . . . just that I hardly know you . . . and . . ."

"And you want a valid health certificate and an engagement ring before you'll risk a good-night kiss?" Message deciphered, I completed his sentence.

"You're exaggerating . . . a little." If smiles were contagious, the manboy would have been quarantined.

"Look," a self-righteous tone of voice supported my argument, "I don't blame you for being cautious about your health. Heaven knows, I am too. But just because we live in the AIDS capital of the world, doesn't mean that you have to crawl under a rock . . . or bury your dick in the sand."

Reid laughed in his Joe Cool way. "So what d'ya do?"

"Play it safe, use your imagination, get off on your fantasies."

"Fantasies?" Reid echoed the word as if I had roused – if nothing else – his curiosity.

I studied the young man's face, lowered my voice by an octave. "White jockey shorts are key on my list."

"Yeah?" Sly, nautical eyes narrowed to slits.

"Wanna split this place and model 'em for me?" A lewd kind of smile settled on my lips.

My world stood still for a silent, awkward moment. Reid looked at me looking at him, then signaled our waitress. "Not tonight."

Heart and hard-on sank hand in hand. I had come so close, so very close. Still, no cigar.

" . . . But if you're not doing anything Saturday night," Reid intruded on my self-pity, "I'd like to invite you to my place for dinner."

A flicker of hope rekindled the flame that smoldered in my loins. "What time?" I eagerly asked.

"Eight o'clock?"

"We have a date!"

Perhaps it was the wine we had with dinner. Or perhaps it was the full moon. But whatever it was, it seemed like the right thing to do at the moment.

We were standing by his living room window when he draped an arm across my shoulder. Before us, a moonlit Manhattan skyline twinkled against a celestial, cobalt canvas. His state-of-the-art stereo was humming some mellow sort of tune. And from the ceiling of his cramped, West Village apartment, a single track light pinpointed its beam on our embrace.

Reid cocked his head, and as though I were a visitor to the concrete island, he pointed out this and that landmark. As I craned to follow his tour-guide finger, our eyes. collided like ships in the night. Then it happened.

Unexpectedly, yet in a romantic sort of way, our lips brushed and parted. The warm wetness of his tongue darted in and out, over and across my mouth. My hands, whether by accident or instinct, reached for his most intimate parts.

Casually, all so casually, I unzipped his fly. Levis crumbled by his side. T-shirt slithered overhead. Hands on hips, legs spraddled, Reid batted his eyes as if to beckon me toward greater temptation.

I was speechless. Inches from my grasp, my fantasy awaited. He was tall, blond and hunky . . . and packaged in Haines briefs.

The shorts hid little, revealed lots. An outline of his thick, long pipe strained to escape the cotton trap. Reid reached for his crotch and stroked the hard knot once, twice.

A round, wet stain soaked the front of his briefs. The thin white sheath clung to the length of his cock, plastered its throbbing head.

My lovemuscle was pumped for pleasure. A single finger

raised to touch his rosy, roused nipple. With snail-like speed, I traced an imaginary line from the crest of Reid's porcelain tit to the peaks and valleys of his rippling abdomen.

As I reached for the prize that was stashed in his jockey shorts, Reid, the arrogant young stud I had dreamed of for weeks, backed away. 'Not yet," he commanded in a firm, seductive voice. "There's something I wanna see first."

"Oh?"

"Take off your clothes."

A flare for exhibition goaded my excitement. Lacoste, jeans, sweat socks, sneakers sailed across the apartment.

"All of them," he specified.

Quite willingly, I lowered my briefs, clasped my rod, and cast it toward the stallion.

Reid feasted on my nakedness; I, on his hunger. A shiny thread of nectar dangled from the tip of my aching cock. My nuts drew tight with anticipation.

The manboy tweaked my rigid nipple as he lined his shoulder with mine. His thick hardness pressed against my groin. The warmth of his breath chilled my spine, fueled my passion and caused my hips to thrust in response.

All the self-control vanquished. I broke our clasp and ripped away his shorts. An angry, one-eyed snake thumped against my thigh, struck with a venegeance. Reid crouched below me. His slick, pointed tongue lashed at my balls.

I moaned with lusty pleasure.

His strong, calloused hand primed my pump while a rapture in wet-velvet played on my glands. Rarely had I seen such talent. Reid knew what to do and I liked what he was doing.

It was as though an avalanche of earthly delights was storming my body. Yet despite my ecstasy, or perhaps because of it, I backed from him, pulled Reid to the overstuffed couch.

"Sit down," I told him. "And spread your legs. Spread 'em wide."

The demigod perched on sofa's edge. I knelt before the phallic altar and studied its magnificence. Jutting from a golden thicket, the obelisk waved for attention. Its long, dark shaft was like a heavy wrought iron bar. Clear, seeping juices glistened from its tip.

As I tugged at the prodigious organ, Reid's scrotum churned between athletic, tanned thighs. The pouch was nectarine-size, fuzzy as a peach, and ripe for eating.

I locked my lips around the sack. Tongue rolling around each ball, my hands were free to explore the firm smoothness of man-boy buns.

"Aaaaaugh!" Reid groaned. "C'mon man! Stop teasing me that way!" His strong, rough hands dug into my shoulders, pushed me away.

My liplock was broken, but my hold remained tight on his flanks. Flesh glowing, mind blowing, juices flowing, I pried his limbs still further apart. From the folds of two perfect cheeks, a bright pink eye winked as though beckoning.

Temptation was great. I licked a finger and touched it to the puckered shoot. Reid squirmed as my merciless probe skimmed the fleshy petals of his rosy bud.

"I mean it, man." His tone voiced no conviction. "Stop teas'n' me an' work on my meat!"

The now-gaping hole nibbled at my finger. I wrapped a hand around Reid's straining stiffness while I persisted in tickling his tush. My own hard member was slashing at air and I could sense the sap rising in its trunk.

Self-restraint tossed to the wind, I jumped atop the stud. My passion-powered tool sawed across the ripples of his washboard stomach. "Fuck! Fuck! Fuck!" I panted. "You're too fuck'n' hot!"

Reid buckled beneath me. Our cocks, like duelling swordsmen, clashed in battle. A flourish of wet kisses pelted my neck as Reid ground his hips against my own. The scent of sex was filling our lungs, goading our rhythm to a frantic pace. We were losing control, humping with wild abandon, and struggling, together, for release.

I flinched as Reid touched some tender, raw nerve. Beads of perspiration dotted my brow. Need, hard and urgent, simmered in my groin.

There could be no more holding back. I clenched my jaw, tossed back my head. And soared to the brink of a new cosmic consciousness.

Jerk

T.R. WITOMSKI

You're Being Careful . . .
But You're Not Ready For the Convent
NO PROBLEM!
Join Us .
at
THE CORRAL
for
HOT SAFE J/O!!
Every Monday and Wednesday
9 p.m. 'til ?????
Admission: $5
Includes All the Beer/Wine/Soda You Can Drink
and
Free Clothing Check

I must have seen dozens of ads like that in the last two years. The age of AIDS is the age of j/o clubs. Like most gay men, I have a terrible fear of AIDS, but unlike most gay men, until recently, I was also fearful of these groups of guys who got together for group masturbation sessions.

Let me explain. Before the health crisis, my sexual behavior, while it wasn't "typical" of the way all gays acted, was representative of a particular set of male homosexuals. I was very promiscuous, averaging about two hundred tricks a year. Since I was a regular patron of the baths and the sex bars, getting it on with four of so different guys a week was quite easy to do. My *being* wasn't devoted to fucking around (I've always held responsible jobs, kept up a circle of good friends, enjoyed an active cultural life), but my favorite hobby was having sex with a lot of different men.

I'm thirty-one now and I've been sexually active since I was eighteen. But I'm still not ready to settle into a serious monogamous relationship. Perhaps that's a psychological hang-up of mine, but I can't see getting "married" just to guarantee myself a steady supply of sex – or even a steady supply of *safe* sex.

With my attitudes, my initial antipathy toward j/o clubs may seem strange. At least to people who didn't go to Catholic schools where the level of anti-masturbation propaganda was unbelievable. According to the priests and nuns, the very worst thing you could do – worse than murder, marrying a non-Catholic, or seeing the movie *Baby Doll* – was masturbation. Homosexuality was literally unspeakable, but "self-abuse" was a fit subject for a three hour sermon. And all those lessons on the evils of "polluting your own body with your own hand" had their intended effect on me. While I loved having my dick buried down some hot throat and getting fucked in the ass, I always thought that jerking off was somehow wrong.

I'm not going to say that I never masturbated, but I used to feel terribly guilty whenever I did. Sex with another person was maybe a sin, but it was a venial one, like stealing a dollar from your father's wallet. But masturbation was a dreaded mortal sin – the type of thing you could burn in hell for all eternity for. And masturbation in front of someone or in front of a whole group of someones – that was worse than raping the Pope.

I'm making my mental block about masturbation sound funny, but it wasn't. I knew it was silly to feel the way I did, but I still felt that masturbation was bad.

As the AIDS crisis continued, my sex life became more and more constricted. For eight months, I was completely celibate – and I thought I would go out of my mind. What made it all the more difficult was that I thought my obsession with sex was depraved. Friends were dying of AIDS and I was chiefly concerned with my own lousy sex life. What a rotten person I thought I was!

Generally I'm a pretty even-tempered guy, but one day a couple of weeks back, all my months of frustration seemed to come together and I snapped. I picked the best place to go crazy too. At work. In the middle of an office full of people, I totally lost control over a minor error a co-worker had made. I yelled at this woman until she was on the verge of tears. My outburst, totally out of character, made front page news on the office gossip hot line; by the end of the day, everybody in the company had heard about it.

On Fridays, I always have a few drinks after work with Gerry, Chris, and Jack; we call ourselves our company's "Gay Union." This Friday, my scene earlier in the day was topic *numero uno* of our conversation.

"Jesus Christ, Vin," Gerry said, "when you go bonkers, you really go all the way. I heard you all the way up on the fourteenth floor. What the fuck's the matter with you?"

"Nothing. I just got pissed off."

"Hell, you've been tense for months. Ain't you been getting any lately?"

I had to laugh. "Well, no, I haven't been."

"So that's why you're so fuckin' tense."

"Gerry, with AIDS around, everyone's being careful. The good old days are gone."

"Bullshit."

"No bullshit for me," I said to Gerry, "maybe bullshit for you. But you got a lover, so you really don't know what's happening."

"I don't have a lover," Chris spoke up, "and my sex life is still O.K. There's hundreds of things you can do and still be safe."

"Yeah, Chris, but you're into all that kinky stuff and I'm . . ."

"Vanilla."

"So what do us vanilla gays do?"

"Jerk off."

"That gets old."

"Not if you do it with a buddy or in a group."

Now Jack chimed in: "There's a lot of new j/o clubs around. I've been to a few. They can be great. You should check one out. If you got off more, maybe you wouldn't be such a bitch. Poor Christine is probably still crying. And since you don't like that kinky stuff, you better hope she doesn't send her husband to beat the shit out of that nasty fag who yelled at her today."

Talking about these clubs with my buddies got me thinking. I guess I could go to one. I wouldn't have to do anything. They didn't *make* you jerk off. What was I being such a Pollyanna about? I certainly hadn't been shy about going to the Mineshaft or the St. Mark's Baths.

Monday night, I told myself, I would go to The Corral. I got as far as the front door when I started to get nervous. So I walked around the block. Shit, this is silly, I thought, I'm acting like I'm eighteen again and trying to summon up the courage to go into a gay bar for the first time.

The Corral is like any one of several dozen Manhattan gay bars. Done in a vaguely Western motif, the main floor features a long bar, a pool table, and several video games. Downstairs is the "sex space" – only now on Mondays and Wednesdays it was the meeting place for the j/o club. (The word "club" is something of a misnomer here. Though other j/o groups do operate like private clubs, restricting admission to members, at The Corral, if you paid the admission, you were a member.)

Even on "club nights" the upstairs remains open for regular business. I decided to first have a drink here and pay attention to the traffic that was moving downstairs to the inner sanctum.

I liked what I saw. Not everyone was a Greek god, of course, but quite a few hunky numbers were heading to the back stairs. My curiosity got the best of me. What the fuck, I thought, finishing my Bud, I'll join 'em even if I don't beat it.

So I paid my five bucks. The – what do you call the guy at the entrance to a j/o club? Doorman or attendant doesn't make it – guy at the entrance asked me if I wanted to check anything.

I verbally stumbled trying to reply.

"First time here?"

"Er . . . yes."

"We're pretty relaxed. Some guys check all their clothes. Others like to keep something on – a leather vest, a jock, whatever. Some keep all their stuff on. But remember, it's j/o only. No cocksucking, no assfucking."

"Right," I said, handing over my jacket.

"Have a good time."

Downstairs, there was a small bar – a new addition to the decor, which had previously been "back room basic." But the biggest change was the lighting. It wasn't bright by any means, but it was a far cry from the almost pitch blackness that had characterized the "old" Corral. Of course, I thought, you've got to see what you're doing. Watching and being watched is a main part of the turn-on of j/o clubs.

The large single room had been divided into a series of smaller areas, arranged like a maze. I grabbed a beer and started to wander around.

In one alcove, two naked guys sat facing each other, their legs entwined, cocks hard, beating off, urging each other on: "Yeah, man, jerk that big dick. Beat that fat ol' dick. Yeah, do it, man. Do it."

My own cock stirred. It knew a hot scene when it was in the presence of one, even if my mind was still playing games: What was I doing here? How could I ever join in? How could I masturbate here? How could I ever be a real member of this club?

I was so caught up in my own thoughts that I almost fell over a guy crouched down on the floor, his hand furiously pumping his cock. Around his neck was a leather dog collar attached to a leash.

The leash was yanked and the man moved out of my way. I saw that holding onto the leash was a huge, bear-like man in full leather.

"Fuckin' dog," the leatherman said to the masturbating man, "you're not supposed to get in *people's* way. C'mon, little doggie, get yourself off now. Take care of your business. Hurry up. I ain't got all fuckin' day to wait for you. Cum, dog, cum."

At first, I was a bit embarrassed at witnessing this scene. But I quickly realized that I was *supposed* to watch this "animal training." These guys wanted me to be there. My brain may have been a little slow at rationalizing what I was seeing, but my cock knew what was going on. It was fully hard now, almost begging to get out of my jeans.

Continuing along my erotic journey, I next came on a scene right out of a wet dream. A half dozen guys were standing around in a circle, their hands working on their hard dicks. What a hot fuckin' sight! A porno film come to life. Their cocks all seemed so huge that I was mesmerized by them. Each guy was pleasuring himself in his own special way, and each individual's pleasure was adding to the excitement of the group.

No two guys jerk off in the same way. And this group was giving me a seminar in the art of masturbation. Three guys were using their right hands, two their left hands – and one dude was using both his hands, pulling on his cock like he was milking a cow. Some of the guys were using long, slow strokes; others were concentrating on their cockheads with short, rapid pulls. Some guys liked it wet, and they'd spit on their hands every once in a while – a natural lube for their manual attentions. They were all breathing heavily, and the smells of their sweat and their passion were like an aphrodisiac to me.

I could feel pre-cum bubbling out of my piss-slit. I was gonna *have to* jerk-off – or else cream right in my pants. I searched around and found a bench in a deserted corner room. Thinking no one would notice me for the couple of minutes it would take to get off, I sat down and rapidly unbuttoned my 501s. My cock practically sprang out, desperately craving relief. As I started to masturbate, my mind raced over the events I had seen, blending them together in one erotic totality. I could feel my balls tightening. Any second now, any second . . . .

"Big fuckin' cock. You got a big fuckin' cock."

Oh hell. What an asshole I was! Expecting privacy at a jerk-off club! My cock started to soften. I couldn't jerk off, couldn't shoot my load if someone was watching me.

"Don't stop man. It really looks hot. You playin' with yourself like that. Really hot."

I looked up at the guy. He was naked except for a pair of work boots. His cock was standing straight out from his muscular body.

Christ, what a beautiful cock! Long, thick, uncut.

"Yeah, I get fuckin' hot watching a hot guy like you beat yer meat."

My cock was back to full hardness. The stud's voice was seductive, sweet music to my ears. But was it enough to let me overcome my inhibitions??

"That's it. Yeah, big cock, big cock, big."

My hand started to slide up and down my cockshaft. Just a few strokes, just a few more. I was getting close, real close . . . . The man stepped closer to me. One of his hands reached into my shirt and grabbed a hold of one of my nipples, while his other hand started massaging his own cock.

"Oh yeah, yeah. You take care of yourself and I'll take care of myself. We know how. Yeah. Beat off together. Watch each other. Yeah, I'm getting ready. Gonna cum good. Cum real good."

I was at the point of no return. I felt my jism travelling up the length of my cock. I looked down in ecstasy as the hot cum shot out of my cock.

"Yeah, yeah. Look at all that cum. Good cum. Good cum. Oh shit, shit, man, I'm going off too!"

The last drops of my own jism were still shooting out when I saw my partner spew out the first ropey strand of his juice. Fuckin' fantastic! And he just kept shooting. I thought he'd never stop cuming. Thirteen years of gay sex and this was the first time I had watched a guy jerk off so close to me.

Back to reality . . . .

"You're a hot man," he said.

"Thanks. You are too." I started to put my cock back into my pants.

"You should leave it out. Show it off."

"Maybe on my next visit here. You see . . . well, that was the first time I ever jerked off with someone watching me."

"And I'm Mr. Benson. But that's cool. We all need our little fantasies."

A couple of years ago, I read an article in one of the gay sex mags on sexual fears. Seems the sexual activity that a person's most uptight about is the one he's unconsciously most interested in. That thesis was certainly proved true in my case. I never thought I'd be totally comfortable and guilt-free about jerking off. But now . . . well, come to The Corral some Monday or Wednesday and I'll show you just what I mean.

A New Man

ROBIN METCALFE

. . . *And I'm goin' to the country, lie, da da da da die . . . I'm goin' to the country, sunshine smile on me.*

An old Bruce Cockburn tune was buzzing around my brain like a pesky fly. I hadn't been able to shoo it away since getting on board the train. There sure as hell wasn't any sunshine smiling on me that afternoon. I was hung-over and my hair smelled like cigarette smoke. Outside the window, stirred up by the wheels of the train, the March snow blew in wisps against the window.

As the train careened around a corner, a sharp pain shot up through my forehead. Goddamn poppers. I'd had a couple of good hits the night before, in a vain attempt to revive some moribund disco tunes. I couldn't understand it, they'd been great songs in 1978. Now I could barely coax my feet through the familiar dance steps. As we pulled into another Annapolis Valley town, a dark wall of shingles slid across the window. My face was reflected in the glass, backlit by the bright lights above the aisle. Demonic. The haggard circles under my eyes didn't help matters. Time to hang up your dancing shoes for a while, kiddo. You're going to the country to take the rest cure.

Somewhere behind me the steel trap door thudded into place and the train lurched forward. A blast of cold air from the vestibule ushered in a shaggy clump of passengers, shaking snow from their overcoats and looking around for a place to sit. I slouched a little lower and pretended to be asleep, my arm flung protectively across the empty seat beside me. The aisle started filling up with people trying to get past the intruders, on their way to the snack counter or the can. A masculine hand drummed impatiently on the seat in front of me. Through half-open eyes I did a quick inventory: crotch – nicely padded; shirt – open over a smooth youthful chest; face – fair and cleanshaven. Kind of young. Probably a student going home for the mid-term break. An uneasy flicker brought his eyes into line with mine, then quickly away, then back again for an anxious half-second before they locked firmly in the forward position. His fingertips flexed and dug nervously into the upholstery.

My mind started calculating possibilities. There was a co-ed washroom at either end of the car. The conductor and brakeman seemed to spend most of their time up front, and there was a take-out attendant somewhere in the rear . . . Shit. Will you listen to yourself. You go down the Valley for a break from the meat market and before you even get there you're cruising again. It's like you're on automatic pilot. What was that switch my Dad had on his '63 Buick? Let the car drive itself? Oh yeah – Cruise Control. How appropriate.

I sighed, and surprised myself how deep and sad a sound it was. Surprised the young guy, too. He shot me a questioning glance before the log jam at the door broke up. The conductor hoisted a suitcase up onto an overhead rack and the abominable snowpeople shuffled forward. I caught a last glimpse of firm round buns in polo pants before the crowd carried them out of sight.

Grabbing my satchel from the seat beside me, I rummaged in it for the detective novel I had brought to keep my eyes out of trouble. The bag seemed half-empty. Usually it rattles with junk: my toothbrush, a squashed tube of K-Y and some condoms in shiny plastic packages – the last a recent acquisition. Be Prepared is my motto. I would have made a great Girl Guide. Except for my toothbrush, this time I had left my mobile drugstore behind for the weekend. I was planning to be a good boy.

At Kentville a three hundred pound woman carrying a see-through plastic shopping bag docked herself in the seat beside me and blocked my view of the aisle. Outside, night was rapidly blotting out the landscape. I shrivelled into the corner of the seat and peered at my novel. My eyelids had begun to droop when the brakeman announced we were arriving in Middleton.

Stepping from the railiner into the slush, I caught sight of Pete and Larry waving to me from inside their rusty old pickup. "God, you look a sight!" said Larry, giving me a brotherly kiss. I settled in between them, the gear shift poking up between my knees. "Yeah," I replied, "when I woke up this morning I felt like someone had stubbed me out in an ashtray." We climbed the dark flank of the North Mountain to the refuge of their farm.

Saturday morning I slept in late, dragging myself down to the kitchen for a late breakfast around eleven. Larry was just pulling fresh bran muffins from the oven. I curled up in the rocker with a big mug of tea and slathered one muffin after another with butter and honey. Content to sit, rocking and munching and sipping, I watched the grey rain dissolve the snow in the garden while Larry chucked more wood in the stove.

After lunch the rain let up and Larry suggested a drive into town. Passing over the hump of the North Mountain and down the steep incline of the other side, we saw farmland spread out like a neat checked cloth across the broad basin on the Valley. Soon we were on the outskirts of Middleton. "I thought we might check out Frenchy's," Larry explained. The white barn of a building where we stopped had the name spelled across the front in colored letters like tumbled nursery blocks.

Inside, the bins were piled high with used clothing, shipped by the ton from the States and sold for next to nothing: a quarter for a shirt, a dollar for a coat. Mostly junk, of course, but sometimes you found wonderful things. Shopping at Frenchy's was one of Pete and Larry's favorite pastimes. During my last visit, Pete had found a pair of silk, button-fly, genuine boxer's shorts. He and Larry must have had fun with those.

To my inexperienced eye, the bins did not look promising, mostly polyester slacks and ugly acrylic shirts. Pete found a teensy little t-shirt he was sure he could squeeze into, and Larry was critically eyeing a Hawaiian number, trying to decide if it was tacky enough to merit consideration. Both headed for the changing stalls at the same time.

I wandered about the store, poking here and there in a desultory fashion, picking things up but not really looking. Around me farmers and housewives were absorbed in a brisk search for something useful. I felt out of place and a little awkward.

A stamping sound near the door drew my attention to a man kicking slush from his boots. His creased brown leather bomber jacket might have seen action in World War Two. I wondered if he had found it here. His dark hair was soft and wavy, just a bit too long to be clonish, although the mustache was regulation issue. There was a gentle look about him as he smiled a greeting to the cashier. Although he could have affected that menacing look which is so fashionable, he had apparently opted to let his native good humor show through. Something about him put me in mind of a librarian. Mild-mannered, as they say. But handsome. He hadn't seen me yet. I orbited around the nearest bin, lifting pieces of cloth and pretending to look at them. With a shock I realized that this section was all women's blouses. Beating a hasty retreat to the men's sweaters, I lost sight of my (would-be) friend.

Not wanting to be obvious in my efforts to locate him, I gave half my attention to the pile of clothes before me. Buried partway down was a dark blue sweater of some promise. The collar was larger than a crew, not quite a turtleneck. A sailor's sweater? Living in a port city has made me a fisher of men. Belgian, Argentine or American, when the navy's in town I'm on the street ogling. Holding the sweater to my chest, I was pleased to note that it retained the contours of the last body it had clothed. Surreptitiously I sniffed it. A trace of the scent, as well. A bit small, perhaps, but . . . worth a try.

Just then the man appeared, a few feet away, his back to me, leaning over a pile of shirts. I had time for a leisurely appraisal of his ass, which was small, round and snug, the way I like it. He was a bit shorter than I am, which is only five seven. His jacket was slung over his shoulder, his shirt-sleeves rolled back to reveal sinewy, surprisingly hairy arms. Although his shirt hung loosely in back, his movements indicated a compact muscular body in good trim. I like small masculine men. I wanted to tumble him into the nearest bin and fuck his hot little ass.

The hunklet (as I had dubbed him) circled slowly around the table and came to a halt facing me. A triangle of white cotton flashed inside the open collar of his shirt, dark wisps of hair spilling over the neckband. At that moment he glanced up and saw me watching him. And smiled. A shyer version of the grin he had bestowed on the cashier. The warm flush that rose to my face was echoed in my groin.

A joyous shriek in the background made us both turn. Pete was pulling a pink sequined handbag from one of the bins and conducting a mock battle with Larry over who had spotted it first. The farmwomen in our vicinity, unperturbed, went on with their digging. Obviously they were used to Pete and Larry. The hunklet, however, after reassuring himself that I wasn't leaving, trotted over to where my friends were standing. They tore themselves away from the handbag and exchanged greetings. Scanning over the heads of the others, Larry spotted me and waved me over.

"Grant," said Larry to the hunklet, "this is our friend Doug. He's down from Halifax for the weekend." Grant offered me a warm handshake and an unedited version of his smile. "Grant teaches elementary school here in Middleton." I felt awkward, being introduced to the man I had just been cruising. Then I remembered the garment in my hand. "I found a sweater," I announced, holding it up so everyone could see. Larry frowned. "Do you think it's big enough?" "Sure it is," said Pete. Grant took the sweater from my hand and examined it with interest. "Look," he said, "it's Navy issue. See the tag?" A yellowed scrap of cloth declared it to be a Sweater, Seaman's. A contract number followed and the size: Small. He handed it back. "Why don't you try it on?" I nodded and stumbled toward the changing room.

The sleeves were much too short. But the main body fit my torso like a glove, emphasizing my chest and upper arms. The navy collar made my neck look thick and butch. I pushed the shrunken sleeves up out of the way, and the effect was complete.

"Well, what do you think?"

"Great!" said Pete.

"Yeah, it's okay," admitted Larry.

Grant looked me over with a sly leer. "I approve." I flashed him what I hoped was a devilish smile.

The next time I returned from the stall, clutching my prize in my hand, Grant was gone. "He had some papers to mark," explained Larry, "but he invited us over for supper later."

"Of course," added Pete, "we don't have to go if you don't want to." A hasty protest died on my lips when I saw his teasing smirk.

Yellow clouds hung low over the Bay of Fundy when we pulled into the farmyard. Larry turned on the gas stove in the little sauna he and Pete had built the previous summer on the back of the kitchen. While the heat was building up I had another cup of tea and leafed through an old issue of *The Body Politic*. Then I hung my clothes on the back of a chair and tiptoed across the cold linoleum to the tiny cedar-lined chamber.

The air was hot and prickly dry in the sauna as I set my bare ass on the wooden ledge beside my friends. Larry dashed a first scoop of water on the grill, and the room thickened with steam. A slick of sweat coated my skin, staining the dry cedar slats with the imprint of my buttocks. The hot air seared the lining of my nostrils each time I pulled it into my lungs. After a second scoop had steamed away, first Pete, then Larry escaped to the cool relief of the porch. Only when the heat had become unbearable did I join my friends outside.

Larry stood like a pink crane at the edge of the lawn, peeing into the weeds. Pete was emptying a bucket of cold water from the rain barrel over his head. It flowed in a glistening torrent down the flattened hairs of his chest and belly and arched from the end of his brown cock. Then he did the same for me. I yelped as the cold shock hit my skin. My body's accumulated heat rolled off into the air in clouds of steam.

We repeated the sequence, sitting in the close dark cave of the sauna, washing old poisons away in a river of sweat, then tempering our bodies in the cold wind. The third and last time we ventured outside, we stood at the corner of the house facing the raw gusts from the sea. The New Brunswick shore was a faint grey smudge on the horizon.

Finally Larry switched off the heat and we lathered up and rinsed off in the tubs of warm water he had provided. I stepped back into the kitchen like a conqueror – my body renewed, my skin clean and taut, my muscles singing. Pete and Larry slipped upstairs for a quick tumble in bed while I had a slow, luxurious shave and began to adorn myself for the upcoming visit.

I decided to wear the sweater I had bought that afternoon, even though the coarse wool itched against my skin. The prickling sensation had a warming effect not to be discounted on a Nova Scotia winter evening, and the tight stretch across my chest showed off my better-than-average pecs. My nipples, I am pleased to say, have a rude habit of sticking straight up through whatever material I happen to have on, and the irritation of the rough wool was enough to drive them into a frenzy. In this agitated condition I arrived in the front hall of Grant's small neat house in town.

The winter chill in the air was more than dispelled by the warmth of our host's welcome. Grant wore a red shirt of the most indecently soft flannel. Unbuttoned almost to his belt, it hung casually open to reveal a virginal undershirt of fine ribbed cotton clinging to the sinuous muscles of his stomach. Shiny black hairs curled over the collar. I forced my attention back to what Grant was saying, about the house – his grandmother's – which he had rescued from an advanced state of dilapidation and restored to Edwardian propriety.

A firm grip above the elbow steered me through the downstairs rooms. Grant spoke animatedly, with large gestures, of his childhood memories of the house, the sorry state to which it later came and his own meticulous efforts to strip away offensive panelboard and to match damaged mouldings. The results were impressive. So too was the eager glow that highlighted Grant's handsome features. I considered how pleasant it would be to kiss his full dark lips, when I was distracted by the advent of supper.

Larrry had warned me that Grant was a vegetarian. How could such a red-blooded man eat no meat? Taking my seat at the oak table, I resigned myself to one of those dreary meals of sodden whole grains that numb the palate in the name of health. It was a pleasant surprise, then, to taste the sweet delicate soup Grant had made from home-grown tomatoes put away the previous fall. The fresh-baked whole wheat bread was a far cry from the dense brown bricks they sell for two bucks at my local health food store. A lustrous Bordeaux made everything slide down nicely. Each time I looked up to compliment Grant on his handiwork, I found his dark brown eyes shining at me across the table. Halfway through the meal a warm stockinged foot nuzzled against my ankle. Shifting my leg to press its length against his, I felt a knot hardening in my groin, and saw Grant make a discreet adjustment to himself under cover of the tablecloth.

After the meal we took our coffee into the front room. Pete and Larry claimed the sofa. I sat on the floor by the woodstove, where I could examine Grant's collection of antique schoolbooks. Leafing through a 1904 speller from Prince Edward Island, I felt his warm breath against the back of my neck. While he and Pete traded local gossip, I leaned into the cove formed by his legs, draping my arms over his knees. Grant's fingers played lightly in my hair. Soon I felt myself getting another hard-on.

Through the next lazy hour of conversation, Grant and I kept in playful contact. By this time we had given up any effort to hide our aroused condition. My friends decided it was time to leave us to our own resources. While Pete was in the hall pulling on his boots and Larry was using the can, Grant came up behind me and closed his arms around my waist. "Staying, I hope?" I reached behind and ran my hands down his slim flanks. "Wild horses couldn't tear me away."

Once Pete and Larry were on their way, Grant pulled me close and parted my lips with a demanding tongue. His mouth tasted of wine and coffee. Then he took my hand in his and led me up the oak stairs. I learned that climbing steps is a new experience when your cock is bursting out of your pants. At the head of the stairs was the bedroom, an antique maple four-poster tucked under wallpapered eaves. Grant turned back the clean covers and sat on the edge of the bed. Pulling me toward him, he pushed up my sweater and nuzzled my belly, growling and nipping at my rising nipples. His fingers explored the long hard ridge in my jeans while he tugged at the zipper of my fly. Peeling aside the flaps of denim, he gently lifted my cock and balls out of my shorts. The elastic waist-band pulled tight against the underside of my groin. I closed my eyes and felt a soft wet tongue lapping at the rigid length of my prick.

We broke apart for a moment to kick off our pants, tossing them onto a nearby chair. Grant unbuttoned his shirt but kept it on, the tail dipping down to skirt a smooth, almost hairless ass. I left my sweater as it was, bunched up above my nipples. Hooking my thumbs under the hem of Grant's undershirt, I slowly peeled it back from his chest until he too stood with his stomach and chest exposed. I cupped a hand around the cool pale medicine ball of his butt. When we stepped together again, our cocks pressed side by side, making a sticky smear across our bellies. Then Grant pulled me down on top of him on the bed.

I love fucking bellies. When I was a kid, the first sexual pleasure I knew was lying on my stomach, rubbing the rough sheets until I came. There's something wonderful about having another man's hard cock lined up beside your own, pressing against your belly. With our pants off and our shirts pulled up to our tits, I felt like Grant and I were a couple of bare-assed boys fucking around.

It didn't take much of that hot hard rubbing, though, before my cock began to feel raw. I cursed myself for leaving the K-Y at home. Grant sat up, reached over to the side table and grabbed a blue glass bottle. "What's that?" I asked. "Milk of Magnesia?" "Olive oil," he grinned as he uncapped the bottle and spread the slick liquid along the length of my prick. Attempting a Quebecois accent, he declared, "I call dees my Cock Salade Supreme!" His warm gentle fingers, slowly stroking my cock, were driving me crazy. "You didn't learn that from Madame Benoit! Anyway," I said, "I thought you were a vegetarian?" "Not in bed, I'm not!" he replied, clasping his slippery fingers tightly around our two cocks.

Wrapping his arms around my waist, he kissed me hard on the mouth and moved to flip me over on my back. I pretended to resist and we wrestled for a minute in a sweet tangle of arms and legs and stiff cocks. Then he had me pinned, straddling my legs. His shirt fell on either side of me as he began to fuck my belly. I ran my hands across the heaving muscles of his back. A rivulet of sweat trickled down the center furrow, into the snug crevice of his ass. My fingers molded themselves around the twin globes, feeling his butt muscles tighten with each thrust. A small horny growl escaped from deep in his throat. As his pumping quickened, Grant's mild-mannered restraint crumbled, until he was bucking with abandon, with a cry like a wild animal. I felt a fast pulse in the vein of his cock, a shudder in the hips, then one two three four hot liquid shots, and a warm gush spreading across my belly.

While Grant collapsed, a panting wreck beside me on the bed, I used his cum as a lubricant and finished the last few strokes on my own cock. My cum blossomed onto my stomach, joining his in a widening puddle that threatened to spill onto the sheets. Grant fetched a small clean towel from the shelf of the bedside table and helped me mop up. Then he curled in the haven of my arms while we recovered the ability to speak.

After a luxurious shower, we returned to the bed and talked for two hours, snuggled together with the quilt pulled up around us. The next morning, after a decadent Sunday breakfast of pancakes and maple syrup, and another tussle on the sofa, Grant drove me back to the farm around one. He joined me and Larry for a walk down to the Fundy shore, then he had to get home to finish marking papers, and I had to get ready to catch my train.

A couple of days later I received a card in the mail. Inside he had written Thinking Of You in large rough letters with what appeared to be mucilage sprinkled with glitter. A closer inspection revealed the distinct smell of dried cum. I propped it up beside my bed. Love, Grant.

SafeSex SlaveSchool

MAX EXANDER

My name is Chad. Six months ago I underwent a very special training. My master, who was new to me then, said that I was worth his time, but he recognized trouble ahead unless we resolved some potential pitfalls. So he sent me to a week-long training program at the "SafeSex SlaveSchool" in San Francisco.

But first I must backtrack. There came a time when I began to wonder: Would I ever take a lover, find a master? It seemed for the longest time that I couldn't connect, couldn't find the sadomasochistic relationship I dreamed about. Eventually it happened that I met Sir Dennis (he prefers "Lord Dennis"), but I also wondered: What manner of sex would we have?

That time of wondering and discovery came in the winter of 1983, that period of transition between the dinosaur of extreme brotherly love which some call promiscuity and the dark, uncertain future. For so long, as I wondered and waited, the notion of a relationship had been confusing and even uncertain – for were we not, at all times, forging many relationships of every kind, those Friday and Saturday nights when nothing mattered but instant physical satisfaction? To take a lover, to find a master – one single man – and to explore not the outside, but the inside – this was not on the agenda before that winter.

But when the warnings of disease and the abandonment of the

baths left one deserted in that night upon which we had all depended for love, one sat quietly at home with the pages of *Drummer* open to the yellow ads, reading them – scrutinizing them – but never picking up the phone or writing a letter. Confusion reigned and uncertainty triumphed as I breathed over those ads and those photos, my hand stroking my cock, my mind dragging those leathermen off the pages and bringing them to life in my room, where they bent me over, rammed their cocks up my ass, pinched my tits, ordered me about, and forced me to jerk myself off and drink my own cum before they would retreat into those pages, now closed, their edges ruffled with moisture.

That prevailed throughout that transitional winter, but last spring – it was really early summer – I sat down at Hamburger Mary's, south of Market in San Francisco, and, with my friend Edmond, confessed through tears that I simply could not live another day without getting strung up, worked over, and *used.*

"You're a mess," Edmond said to me that warm June evening. "Like everyone else in this town – and in New York and Chicago and god knows everywhere I think – you think that your life is over because of this disease."

I nodded. He was right. My life was over if I had to keep living on a tightrope of virtual celibacy. One can go to the gym only so long. I picked at my burger and pushed potato salad around on my plate with my fork. I noticed that the tongs were bent.

"Well, it doesn't have to be like that," he was saying. "Not at all. Look, I went through the same thing . . . "

I interrupted him: "Look, Ed, if you're going to tell me about safesex and masturbating over the phone or joining a jack off club, forget it. I want real sex."

We were silent for a moment, as silent as we could be. The sound system blasted Cyndi Lauper at us. I observed two happy leathermen enter and sit down, their leather creaking as they moved past our table. Their smiles irritated me. Were they going about their business as usual? Had everyone else decided to risk everything and just go on?

"I am *not* going to tell you to jerk off over the phone," Edmond said. "Although it's not a bad idea to let off a little steam . . . but that does tend to get the handle on the phone kind of sticky . . . "

I did not laugh.

Edmond composed himself. "Okay, Chad, out with it. What do you *really* want?"

I shrugged my shoulders and cocked my head as if suddenly interested in the new song by Prince that had just come on.

"Chad!"

I looked at Edmond. "You know, I was just telling you. I want the old days back. I want to go out and get fucked and whipped and all of that. But I guess I do want to find one master to do it on a regular basis, I think I do . . . I don't know, I'm confused.

Edmond smiled. "Try to figure it out some more. Keep talking."

"Well, I guess where I get confused is this: I've always wanted to have a real S&M relationship, but until recently, that didn't seem necessary, because there was *so* much to do – The Caldron, the Slot, the Catacombs, Animals, Sunday afternoons at the Eagle. But always, in the back of my mind, I have to admit I was looking. Then the health thing started, and it seemed like the whole thing was useless. Now I'm feeling like I have to find a master and get a relationship, but even if I did, what could we do? I just don't feel it's safe. But it's the only thing I want."

Edmond was nodding his head, sympathetic and understanding. Our waiter brought cups of coffee which steamed and sloshed onto the table. We poured swirls of cream into them. My appetite returned. I finished my burger and my potato salad and started on the coffee. Even with the cream, it burned the tip of my tongue.

"I understand what you're saying," Edmond said. "But the first thing we all have to remember is that part of growing up is realizing that there is a certain degree of risk in life. Period. Next, we have to decide what is an acceptable degree of risk when it comes to this health crisis. If you don't care, then don't define it. But you're telling me that you *do* care, but that you're just too confused to work out your own definition of what's acceptable and what isn't."

I was working on the hot coffee, blowing across the brown surface, watching it ripple. My full attention, however, was on Edmond. I suddenly felt as if I were in the middle of a therapy session – without the sixty dollar fee. I thought about Edmond for a moment, remembered how we had met three years ago in the laundromat, folding sheets. At first we were fuck buddies, then good friends, still close. Edmond was bright, too smart at times. He was a master craftsman at thirty, creating highly stylized furniture pieces in his loft off Folsom Street. He was small and compact. His eyes were blue intense, his moustache soft sand. He wore a T-shirt that said "This is not a dress rehearsal."

"So," he was going on, "it sounds to me like what you want is a relationship, with heavy, hot sex – you as a bottom, a slave. But you don't want to risk your health."

I shrugged my shoulders. "That's right."

"But you think to yourself: 'I have to offer a master my body to use the way he wants to.' And you're right, that's it. So you need to do that safely."

I shrugged my shoulders again. "Sure," I agreed. "But I don't get it, only because that's just too much to ask – to find a master, to get into a relationship with him, *and* to do it some new, safe way . . ."

He shook his head and cut me off. "It's not hard at all. It's not asking too much. Guys do it all the time."

"But . . . " I started to protest, but he went on.

"Your problem, Chad darling, is that your head is blocking it all up. You know what you want. Go find it. Make the decisions you're making and then turn the fucking inner dialogue off and go do it. Just stop chasing your inner feelings around in circles and be done with it."

I didn't say anything. I was attracted by the advice, particularly about turning off the inner dialogue. Ed was right – I'd been chasing myself around and around, trying to figure out what to do. What I hadn't tried was precisely what he was suggesting – to turn it off and take action, to stop thinking and *do* something.

We didn't talk any more that night. After dinner we had walked down Folsom Street, irritated that the warm June day had yielded to the chill of San Francisco fog. For the next two months after that

I started to go out again, in the evenings. I would put on my leathers, wrap a leather strap around my right arm, and frequent my favorite bars: the Detour on Market Street, the Brig on Folsom, the Eagle on Twelfth. Slowly it dawned on me: I had been in a state of something akin to shock for about a year. Fear had made me withdraw, when withdrawal was unnecessary, even counter-productive. Those summer nights on Folsom Street again – strutting in leather, listening to the roar of motorcycles, enjoying the muscles on display in those hard bars – came back to me with the force of remembered pleasure, a security in habits that had been, and were once again, sources of profound pleasure in the company of a community of men I truly loved.

I realized that I had my life back, the life I had chosen and come to San Francisco to lead, a life of perfect balance which included leather, slavery, and horniness. And I was not the only one. Other men whom I had not seen for awhile were back – safer and wiser – but back nonetheless. And the mood was changed, subtly in some ways, such as the relaxed tempo of evenings at the Brig, the high pressure relieved by responsibility and respect. Communication – which had always been at minimum – was now absolutely necessary, and it fostered a new attitude, a feeling of masculine serenity in stating desires, making terms, and sticking with them.

It was in that context I met Dennis, the friend of a friend. It was late July, a Sunday afternoon at the Eagle. He took me home, stripped me, and worked me over, finally jacking himself off onto my chest and then using his slick semen to jerk me to climax, my lips whispering fantasies: ' . . . to fuck me up the butt and make me crawl across the floor dragging weights from my tits and my balls just to get within sucking distance of that big thing . . . oh god and make me take it everywhere you want, in every position . . . giving me to your master friends for a fuck toy and making me beg for everyone to torture my cock and tug on my balls . . . ' Until I shot my load across the floor.

The "relationship" was much easier than I had thought. Nothing happened. No contract was drawn, no agreements made beyond simple resolutions like "I'll call you tomorrow" or "We'll get together Friday night." One date led to the next, and within a month we both knew that we were having a relationship, as simple as that.

But there was trouble, and Dennis was more aware of it than I. For my confusion – though intellectually confessed to Edmond and myself – persisted in our actual sessions. I begged and pleaded – as part of my submission and verbal fantasy – for Sir Dennis to fuck me, to piss in my mouth, to let me drink his cum and prove our connection. Yet he steadfastly refused to do this. We practiced safesex S&M by default – through his choice and my deprivation. The stronger I became attached to him, the more I wanted what my mind called "real sex."

Finally, one day in early September, a hot, true summer day in San Francisco, the air hazy and the light harsh, Dennis refused to beat me, refused to tie me up and use me. "We have to talk," he said, and we drove to the beach to walk in the cool surf.

We pulled off our shoes and rolled up our jeans and walked along the beach, our toes digging into the wet sand, our feet sinking a couple of inches before the next step pulled them up and set them down again, the cold saltwater rushing in, swirling around our ankles, then retreating again.

"What's wrong, Sir?" I asked.

"You tell me," Dennis said.

But I couldn't answer. I was too afraid, afraid that this was already the end, that I was about to lose him for some reason. In defense, and in romanticism, I etched the scene in my mind: The two of us walking up the beach, the Cliff House far ahead, the glaring ocean to our left, the ugly beach to our right. We walked along the barrier between sea and land. Large Mexican families sprawled across the bright beach towels, radios blaring, open bags spilling potato chips onto the sand. A black couple waded in the surf, the woman shrieking 'But it's too cold!' while her boyfriend pushed her further into the water. A wind that was neither warm nor cold blew past us. I had to turn my head just right in order to hear.

Finally I said: "I don't want to lose you already." Tears came to my eyes.

Dennis looked shocked. "Lose me? Oh, god, man, you've got it all wrong. No, no, no, stop that. That's not what's going on at all."

I took a deep breath and felt wonderful. The great Pacific Ocean curled around my ankles and tickled my toes again. Happy people sat in the sun, contentedly reading fascinating novels.

"Then what is it?" I asked.

"It's the safesex," Dennis said. "You know we're having it, but I know you want something more. You feel incomplete without it, don't you?"

I started to shake my head. "No, of course not, it's just fantasy, that's all . . . " But my voice betrayed my deeper feelings, and I decided to be honest. "Yes, no . . . well, you're right. But don't you figure it's okay now? I mean, it's just the two of us. I'll accept the risk, really I will . . . "

Dennis shook his head. "No, I won't. *I* can't. It's not just you we're talking about. I want to let the leather do the touching – if you'll excuse that! – but I can't fuck you or cum inside you or do piss. I just won't do it."

"But. . ." I said, but I stopped. I didn't know what to say. We reached the cliffs and looked up at the ugly building above us. Dennis shook his head and said he didn't know why they didn't tear it down and reconstruct the beautiful old gothic Cliff House. We turned and walked back the other way.

"Okay," I said after a few minutes. "I'll stop saying those things out loud."

"That's not enough, babe," Dennis said. "I don't want you to be suppressing yourself either. I want to send you to slave training school."

My eyes widened. "Slave training school?"

"That's right."

"I don't get it. That'd be even less, with other masters? Like the old Compound?"

"This is a new one. It's a safesex slave training school. It takes a week. They train you to be safesex slaves, to serve safesex masters. By the time you come out, you'll be so thoroughly well trained you'll beg for me to wear a rubber, you'll be begging for caution and respect. Are you interested at all?"

My dick was already half hard. Part of me loved the idea of the training (I had always wanted to go into the Compound, but never had). Part of me loved Dennis so much I would do anything he wanted to. "Yes, I'm interested," I said. Dennis had seen the lump in my jeans grow into a long bulge.

"Good," he said. "Arrange your vacation for next week. I already reserved your space for the mid-September training session."

I nodded. My dick was completely hard. Dennis took me home and whipped me until sweat poured from my body, and, for the first time in my life, I came without touching my dick.

That is the background for my story. The week which followed that conversation on the beach was filled with preparation. I arranged for a holiday from the office, and Dennis arranged my entrance into the school, though it was extensive. I had to go through two interviews, and those fuckers even wanted a "Statement of Purpose" like I was applying for graduate school or something! Here's what I wrote:

> Sirs, I am a slave with a new master. To me slavery has always meant serving my master in order to satisfy his big dick. Usually this has involved submitting to his orders and taking his sadism until we were worked into a fever of lust that ended with the satisfaction of his big dick, most often shoved up my greasy ass and pounded there until it filled me with hot cum. But my new master – and the new ways we're all thinking about now – make me need your training facility, in the arts of safesex slavery. Please accept my application, Sirs, for the power of slavery is something I can't abandon, but neither will I submit myself to the old ways. I know there has to be a way to do it – to be a hot, obedient slave without enduring any risks to either of us, and I beg to be trained in these methods.

I was accepted, of course, and the next weekend, on Friday at midnight, I was blindfolded by Dennis, put into the pickup, and driven somewhere in the city, I don't know where. I suspect that we were somewhere in the deep south of Market, but it may have been Potrero Hill or even Hunter's Point. I can't be sure, because Dennis drove around and around, turning this way and that, until I lost all track of where we might be, until I began to feel a little bit like I was being kidnapped.

When we finally stopped, Dennis told me to strip before getting out of the truck. I did, pulling off every piece of clothing, my eyes still blindfolded. I was seized by foreign hands then and led through the chill evening into what I later saw was an immense warehouse, converted into a palace of S&M dungeons, rooms, showers, and other necessary facilities.

The first thing I was told to do – and I guess there were about five men giving me orders, Dennis among them – was to display myself to them. They instructed me in a ritual of display which I learned and was often required to perform. I had to turn my body around fully three times, so that whomever was there could see everything I had. Then, after the three turns I was to reach up and pinch my own tits, first the right, then the left, enough to give myself a hardon. Then I was to lift my cock and balls in my hands as though offering them to my observers. Then – and this was the most humiliating part – I had to slap my own ass, once on both sides, really hard, hard enough to make a loud crack and leave a red mark. Then I was to finish by bending over and spreading my ass cheeks apart so that my asshole could be observed, keeping my legs apart so that my balls dangled vulnerably between them. Then, I was to remain bent over like that, legs apart, and to grab my ankles and remain in that position until given orders.

This was taught me in the first evening, and we were all required to do this, sometimes many times a day. After that first instruction session, I didn't see Dennis until the graduation ceremony the next week. I was on my own, though I never feared. The safesex masters were horny and kept me safely on my toes all week.

You never knew what to expect after displaying yourself to them. Sometimes it was a sudden slap, or a lengthy whipping. Sometimes a finger would be shoved up your ass, or a big greasy dildo. Whatever they wanted you to do, they'd just order, and you had to do it, or else you'd get the strict discipline, usually to be tied up spread eagle in one of the large "Discipline Chambers," always filled with tops and bottoms in various stages of disciplinary sessions, and they'd let the guys in the room think up your punishment as they went. If some guy wanted to see my balls stretched really hard, maybe with weights hung off them or with an ace bandage constricting them, then that's what they'd do. So you'd be hanging there naked, and all these guys – anywhere from five to twenty of them – would dream up these tortures. Once, my discipline went on for about three or four hours nonstop! They tied me up and made me beg for every punishment they dreamed up. This one little slave said: "I'd like, Sirs, to see his tits hanging heavy with weights." So the masters made me beg to have that done. Then another guy said he wanted to see me spanked hard with a paddle, so that he could watch the weights hanging from my tits bounce around, and they made me beg for that. But another guy interjected *his* idea that it would be more fun to watch if they could see weights swinging around from my balls, too, so I was made to beg for that. Then they had me all tied up and begging for these tortures, and I had heavy weights dangling from my tits and big lead weights swinging from my nuts, and then they each took turns whacking my butt with this wide leather paddle they had, which set the weights to swinging and bouncing around . . . .

Anyway, we learned a lot about taking torture from our master, and humiliation as well. But there was no structure to the training, unlike what I had expected. I suppose that the lack of structure was actually a structure in itself. What they did was to keep you guessing at all times, and it was a constant series of completely different things, over and over, to the point that you remained in a continual state of horny readiness. And gradually, the message sank in – you were having the hottest slave session of your whole fucking life, completely free of worry or concern over health risks. As that reality settled in, you became exultant at the new world which opened up for you – to be a hot, hot slave enduring heavy S&M sessions with a clear, unfettered mind, an open conscience. It forced you to make an ultimate surrender to them – that of your worry, your fear, your panic. Without fear of the darkest kind, you could trust your masters completely. You could really *give yourself to them*. . . .

They especially emphasized humiliation, making a slave jerk himself off in front of a group of masters, ordering you to tug your own tits and stick a big dildo up your ass and ride it while they jeered and laughed and jacked themselves off. Then, they'd let you cum in your hand and order you to drink your own cum, the only safe cum, they called it, and lick the mess off your hand . . . .

They taught me how to please a master without penetration, surely the crux of the training for me, finally relieving me of my fantasy which conflicted with my will. But twice – and this is curious, because it shifted the issue of penetration to the very heart of the matter which was simply the problem of bodily fluids – twice I was allowed get fucked by a huge master with a huge cock in a rubber. Their position was that fucking a slave was a special rite to be saved for only the most intimate master-slave relationship, once the slave had earned the right to be safely poked and used, but the utter masochism of it was the barrier of the rubber. So you could have your cake and eat it, too, I guess. I was never to have my master's unsheathed cock in my ass. Well, . . . that was one master's version, the one with the ten inch monster who fucked me first. The second fucking was different, a really thick cock, sheathed in glistening flesh-colored rubber. Man, I had to lick that shaft and those low, heavy balls until the whole monstrous arm of a dick was throbbing and needy. Then I had to beg for the *privilege* to be fucked by a master with a rubber on. That really turned me on, getting fucked like that. The utter *caring* of the master, coupled with the freedom of conscience, transported the safesex slaves into unbelievable ecstasy . . . .

Our "graduation ceremony" lasted for two days straight through the final weekend of that week. It was one huge safesex S&M orgy. There were twelve slaves and twenty masters. We were together in the largest hall in the place, completely outfitted with baths, cots for resting, a kitchen, low lighting, and furnished with racks, chains, whipping posts, sex toys, manacles, etc. We slaves were kept naked the whole time, except when leather items were required to be worn.

It was an incredible 48 hours of shifting scenes, some slaves resting while others were worked over, sometimes everyone resting and watching one small, intense scene, humiliating the lone bottom on display for all to observe.

I remember one time when there was only one slave tied up, spread-eagle in the middle of the big room, while the twenty masters went after him. They did everything you can imagine to that kid. I think he was about twenty, maybe twenty-two, blond, smooth, with one of those thick curving horsedicks that some blond kids have.

They tied him up and did it all – humiliated him by making him beg for everything, making him invent and recite slave fantasies for the benefit of all to hear. They jacked him off two or three different times and smeared his own cum on his face, lips, and body, making him lick it off their hands. They whipped him and stuck bigger and bigger dildoes up his butt. They clamped and weighted his tits and nuts. They stuck an electric cattle prod on his nuts. They made him talk dirty to various slaves who jerked off to his fantasies from across the room . . . .

After that, we were given back to our masters and that's when I saw Dennis again. When I saw him later – for I was driven away again blindfolded – I realized how much I had missed him and how much I truly loved him and wanted to be with him. So there I was, safe and sound, or I guess I should say safer and sounder. I've got an insignia to wear on my motorcycle cap or jacket, a special silver pin that has a set of three letters superimposed on a phoenix rising from flames. My pin has "SSS" for SafeSexSlave, and my master's has "SSM" for SafeSexMaster.

The experience had been for me a fulfillment on many levels – to finally attend slave training, to learn the unlimited pleasures of a worry-free S&M relationship, to discover my deep feeling for my master, to resolve my conflicts and regain my lost hotness. All of these were the wonderful outcome of that dark transition when I had sat alone and worried.

Talk To Me Like Lovers Do

JOHN PRESTON

"Hello." [Yawn.]

"Hi."

"Oh. *Hi!*" [Yawn.] "What time is it? 12:30? Is something wrong?"

"No, no, just a sex attack."

"Sex attack? What the hell . . ."

"You know, like a Big Mac attack? When it just comes over you and you have *no* choice but to give in? When your cock is so *hungry* you have to feed it some beef?"

"Oh, yeah? There you are, sitting in the big city, all those men out there . . ."

"All those diseases, filthy amoebas, dirty microbes, deadly viruses . . ."

"Big cocks, gaping assholes, hard tits, open mouths . . ."

"Who cares?"

"You don't? You call me up in the middle of the night and you don't care?"

"All of it's ancient history. All of it. Just something that's not there any more."

"You mean me?"

"Oh, come on, you know I don't mean you. That's why I'm calling you."

"Are you trying to tell me that the simple sound of my voice is enough to make up for all those available men? You live in a city that's founded on the assumption that all men should fuck and suck . . ."

"I live in a world that goes crazy over the sound of your voice."

"Oh? Just the sound?"

"And what it means."

"What does it mean? Come on, tell me . . ."

"It means if I talk to you on the phone I can picture you better than if I'm alone. I can take the sound of your voice and I can *feel* your skin, I can make believe my hands are pulling on those hairy balls of yours . . ."

"What are your hands pulling on?"

"*My* balls."

"That's what I thought. Those hefty low hangers of yours. Just lying there, stretching down between your legs . . ."

"Nah, nah, I'm too turned on. They're pulled way up, *way* up, right to the base of my cock."

"Then you must be hard."

"Sure am. Like I said, the sound of your voice . . ."

"Is it making you *real* horny to talk to me."

"You'll never know."

"Tell me."

"There's this drop of cum sneaking out of my slit. It's pure, just crystal pure. I can just imagine if you were here . . ."

"No bodily fluids . . ."

"Bastard, even on the phone?"

"Even on the phone. Got to clean out that dirty mind of yours, got to teach you some lessons."

"I can imagine some lessons you could teach me."

"I can too. I bet if I was there I'd be doing it."

"What would you be doing."

"Giving you a good lesson in some downhome discipline. Just the idea of your thinking about going out tonight . . ."

"No, I wasn't! Honest, I wasn't . . ."

"You wanted to. You wanted to go out and put your stuff on the street."

"No, man, why would I do that? I have you. Right here, just punch in some numbers . . ."

"I don't want to hear that shit. Get your ass up, right up in the air."

" . . . There, it is."

"Got your legs spread?"

" . . . Now I do, it feels so hot."

"Your balls hanging down?"

"Yeah, they're swaying back and forth. Oh, man I can *feel* your tongue on them. I can feel you lapping away and moving them back and forth, your hot hand's moving my cock . . ."

"What kind of discipline is this?"

"The *best*! Really, the best. You're showing me how hot it is to pick up this phone, punch in your number, get you to move me around, get my balls hanging down, better'n going out, any day, better!"

"You'd rather get me on the phone and pull your big thing, feel up your own balls, feel some air on your bare asshole than go out, get some big hairy chested stud to . . ."

"Don't want any hairy chested stud but you."

"Just 'cause there's all the disease, all the danger . . ."

"No, not for me! Really. For you. Couldn't do it man. I thought about it. I did. I thought about it and I got *sick* about it. Just the idea that . . . But not for me. Me? What the hell, a little danger, a little risk . . ."

"A *little*?"

"But you! I couldn't do that to you. It made me . . . it turned me off. But there I was with that cock of mine, needing it, needing something more than just myself for change, that's why I called. If I heard your voice, got you hot, got you talking to me . . ."

"I'm talking, aren't I?"

"Yeah, you're talking, talking about my big hard cock, getting me thinking about your tongue on my tits . . ."

"You playing with them too?"

"Now I am. I got one in my right hand, pinching it the way you do, got my cock hard in the other, got the phone on my shoulder, got your voice coming through the lines, telling me to get hot, get it off, jerk my cock . . ."

"You getting there? Huh? You listening to your man talking to you? Getting pissed off that you even *thought* about . . ."

"But I didn't do it. Didn't even put on my coat. I just knew that the sound of your voice, the way it'd make me think about you and your skin, your tongue working on my balls . . ."

"No! Your tits. My tongue would be working on your tits. I'd be biting a little harder now, getting a little rougher, 'cause you'd be getting closer. You are, aren't you? Getting closer? I bet your balls are churning now. Just imagine if I was there, the way your tits would feel. I *know* you're not pinching them hard enough. You *know* I'd be doing it harder than you. Come on, *harder.*"

"*Jesus!* Oh, man, you get so close to hurting me. Do you want to?"

"Me? Hurt you? No, no, I just know what you really like. That's all. Now, come on, move your hand and get the other tit, the one that's so soft, that you haven't worked on."

"Come on, that one's tender."

"You let someone else play with it?"

"No, *promise*! Like we said. No one else. But I beat off earlier . . ."

"This is your second time?"

[Pause.]

"It's my third."

"You're that horny! Great. Hot, bothered, needing to hear my voice. Come on, play with your tit. It's not my fault if you overdid it before."

"It just wasn't the same without you. Just beating off alone. I mean, I like to jerk off. But when you're here it's so much better. Oh, man, can't I let up on my tit?"

"No, no, I'm here now, remember? Everything feels good when I'm here. How's that cock coming? Huh? It getting ready?"

"It's just *flowing*. It's just *oozing*. Jeez, if you let go of my tit, if you let me let go . . ."

"Okay, okay, let up on it, just take advantage of how sensitive it is. Go on, wet your finger and run it over the surface, nice and easy, the way I do it when you're so close . . ."

"Oh, *Jesus* . . .! If feels so good. Really. Your voice and my hard cock and my tit all together, telling me to shoot it off . . ."

"*Now*! Come on! *Now*! You want me to hang up? Go away?"

"No! No!"

"Now get that load off. Get it off hot and hard. I want that fucker to shoot up over your head, wet your hair, pump your. . ."

"OOOOooooohhhhh. . . ."

[Clunk.]

"You there? Hey, you all right?"

"Yeah. [Pant] Yeah. I just dropped the phone. God, that was good. Just wonderful. Getting off with you! Man, so much better than going out and getting drunk, taking a chance I might take a chance . . ."

"I told you it'd be good. I promised you you could just call when you wanted to. Like mutual support, you know? Like guys quitting smoking, calling each other up, using each other."

"Yeah. Well. Look, I'm going to see you in a couple days, right? More of that good stuff together? Huh? I got my tickets, everything. Thanks. Thanks a lot for tonight. But I won't keep you. I mean, I'm sorry. I *had* to call. But I'll let you go . . ."

"Hell you will! You're going to stay right on that phone. You're going to tell me every single thing we're going to do when you get here. You're going to . . ."

"It's just that I know you got to get up early . . ."

"Listen to me, asshole. What the hell do you think I'm going to do with this big boner of mine? Huh? You call me up and get me horny and then you're going to drop me?"

"No, no, I'll get you off. I'll get you off now and I'll get you off this weekend. You just hold onto that phone of yours. I have plans for you, stud. I have great plans for you this weekend."

"Yeah, tell me."

"I will, stud, I will . . ."

Inevitable

A Screen Treatment for a Video-film

MACH

SCENE 1: THE BEGINNINGS

1A [Inter: Gym, Gary, Hal, Coach]

The film begins with shots of two young men, in wrestling uniforms, in a junior college gymnasium. We can tell from the way they deal with each other that they know one another very well, are buddies, but are very competitive nonetheless. Gary is working class, with coarser, darker features, while Hal is the cuter, preppier of the two. The two take a college wrestling stance as we see the Coach from the back.

The wrestling match that follows is shown in extreme close-ups which lovingly detail the sweat dripping down foreheads, the chests panting one against the other, and the way a hand is gripping at a jockstrap during a struggle for supremacy in this bout. At the end, Gary struggles hard and pins Hal. When the coach's hand comes down in a dramatic movement, both young men collapse together as if they were lovers worn out from a furious orgasm.

During this we've seen the titles for the film: INEVITABLE.

1B [Exter. Car; Gary, Hal. Night]

Gary and Hal are seen in an automobile at night. Hal is driving this nice-looking used car. From their conversation (no more than six short lines), we understand that they will be parting soon, since each young man has plans to leave this small town where they grew up. Gary is spending the night at Hal's family's home.

1C [Inter. Hal's bedroom; Gary, Hal]

This is the suburban bedroom of a junior college student still living at home. Appropriate pennants on the wall and dirty clothes on the floor. We see the bed from above; the two of them lie back to back. While Gary appears to be asleep, Hal is restless. He reaches into his jockey shorts and jerks himself off, craning his neck so that he can stare at Gary. The shaking of the bed stirs Gary, who startles Hal just as Hal is cumming, holding his breath and trying not to make any sound.

Gary sits up in bed and goes off to the bathroom, trying to hide his erection from Hal.

1D [Inter. Suburban bathroom; Gary]

Once in the bathroom, Gary pulls out his dick and jerks it off, pulling Hal's jockstrap from the gym bag so that he can sniff it while he takes care of his sexual needs.

1E [Inter. Bus terminal; Gary, Hal]

Gary and Hal say goodbye at the bus terminal, where Gary is leaving for the Army. They shake hands awkwardly and almost embrace – but not quite.

SCENE 2 CON GAMES I – SHOWTIME
2A [Inter. "Stage"; Hal]

We see Hal standing awkwardly in a pool of light on a stage. He is looking straight out at us – the camera – and being addressed by the unseen pledgemaster throughout this scene. As part of his fraternity initiation, Hal must first strip naked. While he does so, we hear his voice-over reading a letter he's written to Gary: telling about his loneliness on campus and his hope of meeting "nice fellows" at the fraternity.

Once he's started, the fraternity brothers tell Hal to jerk off for them. He starts out listlessly, nervously. They tell him to really put on a show for them.

2B [Inter. Sleazy motel room; Gary, Sarge, Lefty; Night]

This is a sleazy motel room in a small Southern city (perhaps Jackson, Mississippi). Three servicemen enter, wet from the rain. We learn that they've taken a room for two and smuggled the third one in – the third one is Gary. We hear Gary's voice-over reading a letter to Hal: "I'd really be lost around here if it wasn't for these two great guys who're my pals. We call this guy Sarge because he used to be a Sergeant but got demoted. Then there's Lefty – he's a very handsome guy. They're helpin' me out with pussy-huntin'." During this voice-over, Sarge has taken out a deck of cards and started doing tricks with them. He and Lefty get into some sort of competitive argument, which we see wordlessly. Sarge starts dealing for poker, and we hear the dialogue in the motel room.

Gary protests that he's all out of money and that Sarge and Lefty were arguing which of them was the better poker hot-shot. Sarge off-handedly says they'll play strip poker.

We see an edited version of the progress of the game. All of the men are seen stripping out of their uniforms and down to military issue boxer shorts. But Gary is stripping faster and further than the others. Finally, he's down to just his undershorts and Sarge tells him that a guy has to play one more hand after he's naked. The point of the game, Sarge explains, is that the loser has to "do some crank-pulling."

After the last game, Sarge tells Gary to work on his cock. Gary is a little uncertain, in the company of these supposedly-straight guys, but since he did lose the game . . . . As Sarge and Lefty lie back, with their hands behind their head, and the musty Southern rainfall hits hard against the windows, Gary takes care of his own erection.

2A & 2B
Intercut between the two scenes:

Hal is told by the pledgemaster to talk about his sexual prowess while jerking off. Embarrassedly, the naked collegian invents sexual exploits with sex-hungry females as he fists himself.

Cutting back to the sleazy motel room, Lefty asks Sarge if this is all they're going to get for their troubles, Sarge whispers back that "prize chicken you gotta bring along slow." Gary, as the loser in strip poker, has been told to put on a show for them, jerking off.

We see the two young men (to quote a Christopher Street cartoon) have simultaneous orgasms – but in different cities.

SCENE 3 CON GAMES II – GETTING SOME
3A [Inter. Dorm room; Hal, 2 upperclassmen]

We hear Hal's voice-over, writing another letter to Gary; speaking guardedly of his frat initiation, and how he's beginning to feel uneasy about some of the upperclassmen.

We see a typical dorm room. Two upperclassmen are seated on either side of a film projector, which is showing a 16mm porno film. Hal is squatting between the two seated hulks. While Hal is stripped to just his jockey shorts, the two older collegians are naked from the bottoms of their shirts to their knees. As the two of them get off on the porn film, Hal smears butter on both cocks and jerks them off. As he continues to do so, the upperclassmen remove more layers of clothing, eventually revealing bare chests and then complete nudity.

Then, one of the upperclassmen breaks the silence by saying, "That's too much butter, you're going to have to lick some of it off." After being reminded of a pledge's duty to the upperclassmen, Hal slowly runs his tongue along the length of the slickened cocks.

3B [Inter. Sleazier motel room II; Gary, Sarge, Lefty]

Another sleazy motel room, not unlike the first. The same three servicemen are there, complaining about the fact that it rains every time they get a weekend pass and come into the city. We hear Gary's voice-over explain to Hal that the weather has been very bad and that's made girl-hunting difficult for the guys on their weekends away from the base.

Tonight in the motel room, Sarge challenges him to a race for putting on a rubber. Sarge wins; Gary is completely inept. So Sarge offers to teach Gary; Gary will put the condom on Sarge's cock, of course. And, of course, throughout this the three soldiers are passing around a bottle of bourbon and taking big slugs.

Once Gary has the condom on Sarge's cock, Sarge says that he ought to make use of it and asks, in a completely joking manner, whether Gary's ever been cornholed. Then he starts tickling Gary, who laughs uncontrollably. Lefty joins in and tickles Gary while Sarge pulls Gary's clothes off of him.

Gary is being held down and tickled by Lefty while Sarge places his condomed cock against Gary's ass. Gary stops laughing and tries to pull away, but Sarge lies on top of him and calms him, grunting, "C'mon. Do it for a buddy, huh?" Then he enters Gary, slowly but surely, and begins fucking.

3A & 3B
Intercut between the two scenes:

Intercut between Hal licking on the two frat brothers' cocks until they shoot all over his face and chest, and Gary being fucked by Sarge, while Lefty rubs his cock to orgasm all over Gary's belly.

SCENE 4 GETTING WET
4A [Inter. Tile shower; Hal, upperclassmen, athletes]

We see Hal, in a tiled area, stripped to his jockey shorts, with a small group (2 or 3) of fraternity brothers around him. We hear his voice-over; another letter to Gary: he says that things don't seem to be working out that well with the frat brothers and that he's thinking of quitting the frat. He's heard that if they drum a pledge out of the frat, they get nasty about it.

A blindfold is put around Hal's eyes and his undershorts are pulled off. While one of the brothers attaches something to Hal's back with masking tape, the other two instruct him to jerk on his cock until its hard. He does so. They start to lead him forward.

We cut to a shower room adjacent to a college locker room. There are three large college athletes, stripping out of their basketball uniforms and their jockstraps and getting wet and soapy under the showers just as Hal, still blindfolded, naked, and with his dick erect and in his hand, comes around the tile wall from the other side. He bumps into one of the basketball players. He pulls off the blindfold as he feels large hands on him. The basketball players turn him around; the ink is running down the sign taped to his back: I Want Cock!

In an instant, the three large athletes have Hal pinned to the tile floor of the shower, the water still running, their bodies still soapy and wet. They jerk off all over him, their cum covering his face, belly and crotch.

4B [Inter. Barrack/Military shower room; Gary, soldiers]

Gary's face is seen in close-up, as he writes a letter to Hal. We hear Gary's voice-over: "I'm being discharged but I don't want to tell you anything else about it till I see you. I hope you won't be ashamed of me or . . ." Gary pauses. We see that he's in the act of writing the letter. He rips up the page and crumbles it up. Then he takes his packed Army gear and starts to leave the barracks, but his way is intercepted by a group of soldiers, headed by Sarge and Lefty.

The others push Gary toward the shower room, a dingily painted military place. They rip off Gary's clothes and come at him with scrub-brushes for a "G.I. shower." They rub his skin raw as they start to strip down and shoot their cum on him.

This intercuts with footage from 4A so that we see the cock rubbing against Hal's soapy, wet body, while the soldiers coat Gary's naked body with cum.

SCENE 5 POWER TRIPS

5A [Exter. Frat house; Mailman]

We hear Hal's voice-over in a letter to Gary, saying: "I haven't heard from you in a while. I guess you're busy. I'm leaving college. Can't write more now, but . . ."

We see a letter stuffed in the mailbox of a frat house, as the mailman comes to the door. Close-up on the letter in his hand. We see it was stamped; "Return to Sender" and now the return address is crossed out and marked "No Longer Here."

5B [Exter. Street corner; Hal, "John"]

Hal is standing on a street corner, his worldly possessions in his backpack. He's looking in all directions, not to be coy, but because he's lost. A handsome, built-up man of 40 approaches and asks "How much?" Hal doesn't understand the man. There is a little exchange and then the older man, realizing that Hal isn't playing games with him, backs away and starts down the street. Hal stands there for a moment, puzzled. Then a light comes to his face and he runs down the street, after the man, calling out, "Hey, wait!"

5C [Inter. Corridor; Gary, 2 guards]

There is a close-up of Gary's face. He looks like he's been in a fight. He is being led down a corridor by two prison guards – one black and one white. From either side there are hoots and sexual threats from the other prisoners. Gary looks furtively from side to side, trying not to show fear.

5D [Inter. Prison Cell; Gary, 2 guards

Gary is led into a small cell. One of the guards tells him not to look so worried; he's just in on a drunk and disorderly for a few days and will be closed into this small protective custody cell so none of the other prisoners can get at him. Then the guard gives Gary a meaningful pat to the rump.

5E [Inter. Fashionable apartment; Hal, "John"]

Hal is looking around at the fashionable apartment of the 40ish bodybuilder who's paying for his services. The older man tells him he rarely finds someone as nice- and cleancut-looking as Hal selling it. Hal assures him he hasn't done it before and the older man laughs. When Hal asks why such a well-built man pays for it, the bodybuilder tells him he's highly paid, his time is worth a lot to him, and he likes to get exactly what he wants.

Hal chuckles nervously at this. The older man grabs up some clothes from a drawer and hands them to Hal, directing him into the next room.

There is a quick cut. Now the older man is wearing a sweatsuit. Hal is in a Catholic school gym uniform and is over the "Coach's" lap. The shorts are pulled down and Coach is spanking Hal hard on his bare butt, the cheeks framed by his jockstrap.

5F [Inter. Prison cell; Gary, 2 guards]

Gary is asleep in his darkened prison cell. He lies on the cot in his undershorts with a thin blanket pulled partially over him. He doesn't stir as the door to the cell is unlocked and slowly opened. It's the two prison guards come back.

Before Gary can move, he is pounced upon by the two of them. A pillow is put over his head and each wrist is handcuffed to a corner of the bed. His shorts are ripped off him as a prison guard mounts him from behind.

"You got any rubbers? I don't want my wife to smell a boy's asshole on my dick," the first guard says to the other. So saying, they both sheath their cocks and take turns fucking Gary, helplessly cuffed to the bed.

5G [Inter. Fashionable apartment; Hal, "John"]

The bodybuilder, naked now, is on top of Hal on the floor, telling him: "C'mon, it'll be safe. I've got a rubber on." Hal is still reticent as the man says, "$70! $90! $100! I know you could use $100!"

At this, Hal's look changes. "Be gentle with me, Coach." Those are the words the man was waiting to hear. He fucks Hal.

Intercut with footage from 5F, so Hal and Gary are both being fucked simultaneously.

Cut to Hal putting his clothes on, taking the hundred dollars that the older man left on the dresser. The man tells Hal that someone as cute as he is would be safer and command more money if he worked through a service. He shows him a newspaper with ads for escorts/masseurs.

SCENE 6 TRANSITIONS

6A [Exter. Suburban home; Gary, Hal's parents]

At the door of Hal's parents' house. Gary is being greeted at the door. He's told that they haven't heard from Hal and are worried about his whereabouts.

6B [Inter. Hal's apartment; Hal]

Hal is on the phone to Gary's parents. He's being told that they threw Gary out of their house when he tried to return home. "He's no son of ours no more." Click.

When Hal hangs up the phone, it rings immediately. It's his hustling service with a call for him.

6C [Inter. Carpentry shop/Locker room; Gary, workman]

Gary goes to work in a carpentry shop, where we see him working with the other laborers and overhear one saying that although they don't know anything about Gary's past, he keeps to himself and works hard.

The men have to change out of their greasy work uniforms and shower in a cramped, filthy company locker room. When one workman makes a passing comment about Gary being "queer," Gary springs up and attacks the man so violently the rest have to pull him off. "Don'cha have a sense of humor?"

6D & 6E [Inter: Hal's apartment/shop/locker room; Hal, Gary, client, workmen

We see three different shots of Hal intercut with three different shots of Gary.

First Hal is seen posing and oiling himself while a "client" jerks himself off in the background. Then, Hal is seen opening packages of new clothes he's bought himself from fashionable boutiques. He pulls on an expensive shirt that shows off his chest very well. And finally, Hal is seen working out with weights, admiring the definition he's getting in his chest.

Intercut with this, we see Gary at work with the other laborers: First he pauses to help the man he had the run-in with in the locker room — there's a friendly smile between them. Then we see Gary chug-a-lugging a bottle of beer with the guys, spitting most of it up, and them all laughing together. And finally we see Gary, in the locker room again, snap his towel at the bare ass of the guy he'd had the run-in with.

SCENE 7 RITUALS
7A [Inter. Another apartment; Hal, Rich Trick]

Hal, on a call as a hustler, enters a fabulous looking foyer, greeted by a handsome, perfectly sculpted man. They both smile and Hal (quoting his first John) says, "Don't tell me: Your time is worth a lot and it's easier for you to pay for it and get exactly what you want."

Quick cut to Hal, in a butler's uniform, and the Rich Trick naked in a sunken bathtub. What follows is a scene of the butler (Hal) giving the Rich Trick a complete body shave, all soapy in the tub. It ends when Rich Trick shoots all over the front of the butler's uniform.

7B [Inter. Locker room; Gary, workmen]

The men of the shop (4 in all, including Gary) are in the locker room way after hours, drinking heavily, and smoking a little pot. They're having one of these "Oh, yeah?" "Yeah!" arguments, without making any points. One of them whips out his dick and declares a measuring contest. All dicks are coaxed out and hardened by hand by men who are keeping their pants and shorts around their knees. Then they're measured one against the other.

The man with the shortest dick challenges the other guys to a shooting contest, to see who can shoot cum the furthest. All of them are in a circle, jerking off at each other and eventually shooting.

7C [Inter. Musty bedroom; Hal, another client]

There is an unseen old man in a bed as Hal enters the room, cassette player under his arm. He sets up in a professional manner, occasionally smiling toward the bed. Then he adjusts the lights, turns on the music, and does a very sexy striptease for the unseen old man.

7D [Exter. Car; Gary, workmen]

As they drunkenly pile into a car, the four laborers insist that they didn't do anything queer and that none of them would ever do anything queer. To reassure themselves they're going to beat up queers. They have trouble starting the car but are soon on their way.

7E [Exter. Street; Hal, Gary, workmen]

Hal has just left a house and is walking jauntily down the street, money in his pocket. Someone approaches him on the street, a little unsteadily, and says, "Got a light?" Hal pauses and is then pounced upon by three other figures, all enraged and all shouting epithets at him.

When Hal looks up, he finds himself face to face with Gary. For a moment everything is still. Then one of the others grabs Hal by the arm. Gary intervenes, "Who said you could lay a finger on him, Pig shit?" Gary and Hal fight the other three and make short order of them, bashing them in the guts and sending them wailing down the street.

Then Gary and Hal are left together on the street, panting for breath, not quite daring to touch, and finally squeezing their hands together as tight as they can.

SCENE 8 LOVE!
8A [Inter. Hal's apartment; Hal, Gary]

The two of them awkwardly enter Hal's apartment. Gary is surprised at how expensive it is. Hal doesn't want to talk about it. They both now have pasts they don't want to talk about – very different from the last time they saw each other.

Finally, when they can't help it anymore, they fall into each other's arms and kiss as if their lives depended on it. They can't get enough of touching each other, of holding, squeezing, feeling, finding out. They are pulling off each others' clothes, and as each article is removed there is licking, exploring, touching, biting. An ear is nibbled. A toe is sucked. Nipples are licked, tickled, bitten and blown upon. Hal pulls a hair out of Gary's chest – with his teeth.

Then Gary asks Hal if he wants a rematch on the wrestling match they had when they last saw each other. This time they wrestle nude on the floor. It's winner take all – all of the loser's body. When Hal pins Gary, their bodies glued together by sweat, Hal stays right where he is and fucks Gary between the thighs, the two of them passionately touching and fondling all through.

The sex grows increasingly erotic between Gary and Hal. During this we cut away to fantasy sex as the fucking moves to the sky/to a video game/to the front steps of the 42nd Street Library/to a palace. And then they're having sex back in the bedroom Hal had in his parents' house, back in that bed that smelled of college jocks.

Back in Hal's present day bedroom, the two of them are lying, tangled together, in the pleasant afterglow of sex. Gary begins saying, "You know, all those years ago, I wish I had . . ." but Hal silences him. "The past doesn't matter. It's time to think about the future." And with that they go to sleep together.

THE END

A Nice Jewish Boy From Toronto

MARTY RUBIN

I fled southward from the leaden-grey overcast skies of an interminable Canadian winter, seeking to recapture my lost youth and find new sexual adventures. The promise of hot sun, warm sandy beaches, and slender, smooth-limbed, sun-bronzed boys drew my winter-encrusted soul like a magnet.

The week before I left, I had experienced a bizarre sexual encounter which, although delightful, had been profoundly disturbing, leaving me with the evocation of a high-school passion now thirty years in the past. I still couldn't banish from my mind the taste of Jerry-Boy's lips or the electric tingle of his hot young breath against my neck as we awakened, limbs intertwined, to our three brief mornings of frosted windows and the bubbling aroma of hot brewing coffee.

Toronto in midwinter is a Dantean vision of hell frozen over. The clustered skyscrapers of the vast and futuristic city look like giant icicles. Dirty frozen slush clogs the traffic-choked streets and freeways. Offices and factories are decimated as the winter colds and flu make their rounds. Normally a cheerful, happy, polite, insouciant, gregarious city, in winter a sort of cabin fever sets in as people draw into a frozen, alienated silence. Bundled in winter garments, they sullenly crowd aboard the packed streetcars and subways, driving having become impossible. At my apartment building, I hadn't moved my car from the underground garage in weeks except to run the engine occasionally. My motorcycle stood in its designated space, greased under its winter wrappings. Occasionally I would visit it and talk to it.

On Friday nights, the motorcycle club to which I belong hosts a bar night at one of the local establishments. It was late on such a Friday night in February when I left the Leather Corral and headed north on Yonge Street to walk the few blocks home. Except for an occasional after hours restaurant, the normally busy thoroughfare was shut down and deserted, the store windows dark. The wind howling in from the north was bone-chilling, even though I was warmly clad in lots of fur and leather. The promise of a blizzard hung in the air like a menace. Even most of the street boys had found shelter, although a few desperate specimens still roamed the street or huddled in doorways, trying to cruise up a money trick for the night. At this point, most of them would have been glad to settle for a warm bed, some breakfast, and subway fare.

Ah, the street boys of Yonge Street! They are like no other street boys in the world. Sharp-eyed pool hustlers from the city; hunky rosy-cheeked farm boys from the prairie provinces; pasty-skinned, ferret-eyed French-Canadian boys from the French-speaking enclaves of Quebec and parts of the Atlantic provinces, barely able to speak the mainstream English of the country, trying to make their one big score in this vast, multi-lingual, multi-ethnic city where French is seldom heard. And how quickly they all become hardened and streetwise, ready to sell themselves to anyone, for any purpose, to do anything for the money to survive another day. In the dead of winter, they hitch-hike across the Trans-Canada highway, giving it up and heading home, or back to the city for another desperate try. They clog the shelters and the half-way houses; they dream ambitious dreams; they get themselves killed over dope or money or a john. There is always the option of going to work, of course, but the streets, for them, have become a way of life.

Ordinarily I make it a practice to avoid the street boys, unless they come well-recommended and introduced. After all, they have so little to offer, nothing to lose, and at times can be very dangerous. So it was to my own surprise that I stopped to talk to the boy who had just stepped out of a doorway to make his approach.

He was like no other street boy I had even seen on Yonge Street. For one thing, I sensed that he was Jewish, like myself, and there is no reason, in Toronto, for a nice Jewish boy ever to have to hit Yonge Street. For another, he was beautiful, rather than starved and ragged-looking, with dark-gold, almost cinnamon skin and dark-blond curly hair protruding from under his winter cap. But it was the eyes that transfixed me: bright and alive with intelligence, and, I suspected, capable of merriment and humor. There was absolutely no trace of begging or humility in his voice when he said,

"Hey, man, I sure could use a hot cup of coffee."

I looked directly into his face, so much like that beautiful face that I had seen so many times before, long ago, had known so well, had loved so deeply. "What the hell are you doing on Yonge Street, kid?" I asked.

"Trying to find a warm place to crash."

"Let me rephrase the question. What the hell are YOU doing on Yonge Street?"

"Freezing my ass," he replied. "Do I have to give you my whole life history, or can we go someplace warm?"

Not wanting any misunderstanding, I asked him right up front, "How much money were you expecting, kid?"

"I didn't say I was looking for any action. I just need to get warm." Then he added, "Maybe we can work something out later."

"You'd better come along to my place," I said. "We can talk there." I remember wondering why I didn't just tell him to fuck off. I guess it was that face of his, a ghost out of the past.

He shrugged indifferently and fell into step beside me. We huddled against the wind and did not attempt to speak until we had passed the Wellesley Street subway station and turned east off of Yonge to enter the lobby of the luxurious high-rise where I live.

"I'm impressed," he said.

In the elevator we stood apart from each other; I made no attempt to touch him, but merely observed him. He was tall, almost my height, and slender without being skinny or emaciated-looking. Despite my usual paranoia about street boys, I felt absolutely no apprehension or fear.

The elevator stopped at the 28th floor, which consists of just two penthouse suites. I unlocked my door.

"No *mezzuzah* on the door?" he asked.

"No *mezzuzah*," I replied. "I'm a devout militant atheist."

"But Jewish?"

"Very much so. By the way, what's your name, kid? You might as well give me your right one, because I've been known to check I.D. when I bring a strange kid home."

The kid stuck out his hand. "Jerry Stoltnick." That was when I knew for sure.

"Jerry Schwartz," I introduced myself. "Two Jerrys. Make yourself at home. I'll hang up your coat." Under the shabby army-surplus overcoat he was wearing the standard Yonge Street hustler uniform: tight levis, cheap dress boots, and a cheap but fancy-looking imitation-silk shirt. He looked over the apartment appraisingly, the library of books, the paintings, the furniture, the *objets d'art*. I flicked a switch by the south picture window and the drapes drew apart to reveal the sparkling wintry expanse of the city stretching southward to the lakeshore.

"You must be doing okay for yourself," the kid said.

"Not really," I replied. "In fact, not well at all. It's a long story."

"Maybe some day I'll listen to it. Right now, how about getting me something hot to drink?"

"I'll fix you some coffee. And a brandy. You're shivering."

When I returned from the kitchen, unworried, for some reason, that he might pocket a valuable or two, he was right where I had expected him to be: poring over the bookshelves. He had a copy of the *Essays of Montaigne* in his hand, which he quickly replaced with a guilty look as I brought in the tray of coffee cups, coffee pot and brandy glasses. Aha, I thought. Caught you being intelligent! I poured him a cup of coffee and a large brandy.

"L'Chaim," I toasted.

"L'Chaim," he responded. "I'm glad I ran into you. How about calling ourselves Big Jerry and Little Jerry? Otherwise I might think I'm talking to myself."

"Let's make that Jerry-Boy and Jerry-Sir. I'm rather sensitive about the word *big*."

"I have this fantasy about hot older leather dudes," he said. "To me, they're *supposed* to be big. At least, that's the way I've always fantasized them. Big and bearded, like you."

"You still haven't told me what you were doing on Yonge Street."

"I dropped out," he replied. "Dropped out of home, dropped out of school, dropped a little acid. Anything else you want to know?" Suddenly a fit of shivering seized him as the brandy hit. "God, it's cold out there!"

"Why don't you grab a hot shower? Or a hot tub. You'll find a nice warm flannel robe inside the bathroom door."

"Thanks," he said, and disappeared into the guest bathroom.

Twenty minutes later he reappeared, carrying his street clothes. When he sat down in the recliner, the robe fell partially open and I could see his beautiful smooth velvet thighs and his gorgeous young cock, the biggest I'd ever seen on a boy of my own ethnicity. Even bigger than . . . . He became aware of my gaze and drew the bathrobe together modestly.

"Jerry Stoltnick, eh?" I said. "Are you any relation to Al Stoltnick?" I might have said, Al Stoltnick, the millionaire real estate developer.

"I suppose I should say no, since you just picked me up on Yonge Street, but what the hell. He's my dad. Why, do you know him?"

"I used to. We were in high school together."

"Everybody claims to have gone to high school with my dad. What high school and what was his nickname?"

"Harbord Collegiate – it was all Jewish then, not Italian and West Indian. His nickname was Socky. Socky Stoltnick. From his amateur boxing. Sock-it-to-'em, Stoltnick."

"Okay, so you know him. Maybe he wasn't an asshole back then. That's all over with now, as far as I'm concerned." He took a sip of his brandy, and a sip of hot coffee. "Are you a millionaire too, like my dad?"

"I don't have a pot to piss in, kid. I just broke up with my lover after five years. Name of Alistair. He met somebody young and cute and they went off to the United States to live. Houston, Texas, actually. He had all the money in the family. But he was decent. He paid up the rest of the lease so I wouldn't be stuck with an apartment I can't afford. The lease has six more months to run and then I'm on my own."

"What do you do for a living, besides *kvetch*?"

"*Kvetching* is how I make my living. I'm a writer."

"Best-selling?"

"Never. Like most failed writers, I survive by writing copy for ad agencies and small publishing houses."

"You're not a failed writer. You just haven't made it big yet."

"Thanks, kid. Now tell me why you dropped out of high school."

"I didn't drop out of high school. I was a sophomore at the University of Toronto."

I was surprised. "Aw, come on, Jerry-Boy! You can't be over nineteen."

"Eighteen. Just barely. So, I'm a prodigy. Actually, I'm a genius." He said that without an iota of bragging, in fact almost self-deprecatingly, the way one might say, I have a bad heart murmur, or I have a high blood-sugar level.

"What were you studying?"

"Liberal Arts and Humanities."

"Why?"

"Because it pissed off my dad. As I said before, he's an asshole. He wanted me to take business courses and make a million dollars like he did, so I did just the opposite. Now I can quote Chaucer and Keats line by line and order dinner in four languages, but I don't know a damn thing about making a living. It drives him up the wall. He says he hates poetry."

Oh, Jerry-Boy! I wanted to tell him. He used to *love* poetry! We used to read poetry to each other. We even used to *write* poetry to each other!

"And music. I have a minor in music. I have this fantasy of being a composer and starving in a garret in Paris for years and years, writing symphonies and concertos that never get performed. My dad says he can't stand classical music."

Oh, Jerry-Boy! I wanted to tell him. Your father and I used to hold hands at the student symphony concerts at Massey Hall when we were kids! In the dark, where nobody could see. And once, when they were playing Tchaikowsky's *Pathetique*, we both had tears in our eyes and leaned over and kissed each other, quickly, as though we'd bumped heads by accident. God, what dreadful sentimental schmaltz we used to love best in those days! Not Mozart or Brahms or Bruckner. Imagine, the *Pathetique*! But we were both sixteen, and so much in love.

"He's into all this macho shit," said Jerry-Boy. "Wants me to be a big athlete. He knows I'm gay and he can't stand it. The very thought kills him."

It didn't kill him thirty years ago, I thought. Afraid that I might cry, I picked up Jerry-Boy's street clothes. "I'll hang these up for you," I said, trying to fold the levis carefully so that nothing would fall out of the pockets.

It didn't work. The wallet fell out, and from it, money and credit cards.

I couldn't believe the kid had ripped them off, so I picked them up and looked at them. Jerry-Boy stared at me in horror as I examined them. "Leave those alone!" he almost screamed.

It was no rip-off. The credit cards matched the Province of Ontario driving license, and the driving license matched the beautiful boy who was sitting in my recliner.

"You phony," I said, now very angry. "You could have checked into the best suite in the Royal York! And you're out there hustling – when all those hungry kids really *need* a meal and a place to stay? Why, Jerry-Boy? WHY? Were you writing some fucking term paper or something?"

"I had this fantasy," he replied, shamefaced. "I always wanted to know what it would feel like to be a street hustler on Yonge Street in the dead of winter."

"So you grabbed the first dude who came along."

"That's not true!" he protested. "I waited until the *right* dude came along!"

Why me? I thought. Of all the two people who had to connect on Yonge Street!

"You mean until the first piece of leather came along! God, I hate rich, spoiled little brats! I ought to smack the shit out of you."

He looked startled. "You wouldn't do that, would you?"

"You think not? You're the one who was out there cruising leather; you must know I *like* to smack kids around! Especially rich, spoiled little J.A.P.s!"

His eyes brightened with curiosity. "Why do they say Jewish American Princess, even though we're in Canada?"

"Probably because J.C.P. would be unpronounceable." I stood over him as he sprawled in the recliner. "Jerry-Boy, I really hate being made a fool of."

"But I didn't mean to do that, Jerry-Sir! And I wasn't lying about one thing – I really did drop out of school! Hey, you wouldn't really hit me, would you? Come on, man, don't stand over me like that, it makes me feel threatened! I don't like anyone to make me feel threatened! Hey, listen, just don't get ideas, okay? If you even try – if you strike me, I'll call up Gertrude and Al – that's my mom and dad – and they'll get you good! I'll tell Al to sue the hell out of you!"

That was just what I needed. I grabbed him by the hair and slapped him hard across the face – once, twice, three times – then slung him back in the chair. His eyes were bulging wide and his beautiful mouth hung open and slack-jawed in shock. After a moment he spoke.

"Nobody ever hit me before," he said quietly. "In my whole life, nobody ever hit me before! Wow! It was an – *experience.*" He gazed at me with what I can only describe as pure new-found adoration.

"Evidently," I replied, "somebody should have." I squeezed his shoulder reassuringly. "Come on, kid. It's getting late and we both need some sleep. Let's go crash out."

"Okay, Jerry-Sir. Just promise me one thing, please."

"Don't tell me you've got a migraine! Just how much of a fucking J.A.P. can you possibly be?"

"I don't have a migraine. I just want you to promise me you

won't try to fuck me, okay?"

"Look, kid, if I wanted to I could simply overpower you and rape the hell out of you. Surely you realize that."

"You won't," he said confidently. "There are rules to every game, and you're not about to break yours."

"Now, how can you possibly know that?"

"I know. You'll fuck me when you know that deep down inside I really want to be fucked. You won't rape me when you know I'm just not ready for it."

"You're very perceptive."

"I have a minor in psychology. I have this fantasy about being a great bearded psychiatrist in Vienna. Now, listen, Jerry-Sir, before you take off that gorgeous funky leather vest, if I'm not too heavy for you, why don't you carry me to bed?"

"Don't tell me," I said. "Let me guess. You have this fantasy about being carried off to bed by some leather Daddy."

"Yes!" he exclaimed delightedly. "Naked and helpless in your brawny arms!"

"Oh, God," I said. "Who the hell writes your scripts? All right, kid. Stand up."

I pulled the flannel robe off him as he stood in the middle of the living-room, slender and beautiful. His musculature was well-defined, but not over-defined. With that smooth, olive, almost Mediterranean skin, the curly blond hair, and those intelligent, almost feline, green-gray eyes, he was the most beautiful boy I'd ever seen. Except for his father, of course, when we had both been sixteen years old.

With a little effort, I picked him up in my arms. He clung to me in rapture. By the time we got to the master bedroom, I was breathing just a little bit heavily.

"You really should work out more," he said, and then kissed me real hard on the mouth. Gently, I lowered him to the bed and tucked him in. Then I undressed and lay down beside him.

Jerry-Boy lay cuddled in my arms, our legs intertwined. "Can we just cuddle this first time? No sex?"

"If you insist."

"I have this fantasy. I've always wanted to be a leather slave.

Can I be your slave boy? Will you take me around wearing a collar and leash?"

"What in the hell would you know about being a leather slave, you little snot?"

"I've read everything I could find on the subject," he replied. "I buy all the big leather magazines every month, and I've read all the top leather writers. There isn't a night that I don't fall asleep thinking about it. Or jerking off about it."

"I hate spoiled little rich kids," I said. "You've done nothing to merit the privilege of being my leather slave. In fact, very much to the contrary."

"What would I have to do? I'll do anything you want." His lips nuzzled my ear. "I hate to admit it, but I liked it when you hit me."

"Tomorrow's Saturday. I don't have to go to work. If you really think you can handle it, we'll get in some solid, intensive training. Then if I think you've earned the privilege, I'll take you with me to the beer bust at the Leather Corral on Sunday afternoon."

"Then I can stay with you?"

"Only until Monday morning. When I'm working and trying to write, I don't need any distractions in my life."

"I wouldn't be a distraction in your life, I could give you motivation. I have this fantasy about playing Elizabeth Barrett to your Robert Browning."

"You have a soap-opera mentality," I said, "even if you are a genius. Jerry-Boy, have you ever actually had real sex in your life?"

"Oh sure," he replied. "Two years ago, with my first cousin Hermie. But that was different; we'd grown up together and neither of us had been with anyone else, so we weren't worried about catching anything from each other."

"And what did you and Hermie used to do?"

"We used to fuck each other all the time and once in a while we'd blow each other. It was really neat." He paused reflectively. "You know, it's funny. There seems to be some bourgeois fallacy that nice Jewish boys don't fuck around with each other the way Gentile boys do."

"But we know differently, don't we?"

"Hey, nice Jewish boys fuck around with each other just as

much as anybody else. The only difference is we tend to intellectualize about it a lot more."

"Nice Jewish boys intellectualize about it if you ask them to pass the butter. What happened with you and Hermie?"

"His folks moved to the States and he went with them. I love the States. I've been to New York and Florida and California. Have you been to the States much?"

"I've lived and worked in the States most of my life."

"There! You see? You know how it is down there. That's why we can't have sex tonight."

"I see. You mean you really want to have sex, but you think we mustn't have sex. Is that what you're saying?"

He squeezed tightly against me. I could feel his huge cock throbbing against my thigh.

"My cock is raging for you," he said. "Is that wrong?"

"I think it's great!" I replied.

"See, I have these top and bottom fantasies. I want to be your slave boy, but at the same time I want to be your top. What does that mean, Jerry-Sir?"

"It means that some day you'll make someone a perfect lover."

"In the meantime, do you realize what could happen if I were to fuck you?"

"You mean if I were to let you have that privilege, which I very much doubt that I ever would. Yes, I do realize what could happen. You would have one hell of a climax. So would I. Hopefully, simultaneously."

He moved his head and nuzzled my nipple, biting it slightly. "That's not what I meant. I could get herpes. I could get hepatitis. I could get syphilis or gonorrhea. I could get non-specific urethritis. I could even, God forbid, get AIDS!"

"But Jerry-Boy, I don't have any of those things!"

"Are you sure? How long has it been since you had your last medical check-up?"

"About three months."

"And how long since you last had sex?"

"About two days."

"And you've been getting plenty of action?"

"I do okay for a man my age," I admitted. "I don't always get as much as I think I want, but I do get as much as I can actually handle."

"There! You see? And you *admit* you've lived in the States! So how could we possibly have sex?"

I sighed wearily. Then I rolled him over onto his back and took him in my arms, kissing him gently all over his face and his neck. He clung to me tightly. "Please, Jerry-Sir, don't."

"Relax, kid. I'm going to give you some much-neglected sex education. I know you've done a lot of reading, but you don't really know very much. You have to use a little imagination. *Voila!* I am about to give you a lesson in safe sex. Do you want sucking or fucking first?"

"First the appetizer," he replied. "Then the main course."

By way of response, I took his enormous cock in my mouth. Or at least I tried. I worked on the head of it, very gently, massaging it with my tongue until I felt him come throbbing to the very edge of climax. He had taken my cock in his hand and was fondling it slowly, keeping me hard and ready.

"Now the fucking." I straddled him as he lay on his back and then lowered myself until I was lying on top of him. "Am I too heavy for you?"

"Yes," he said. "You need to go on a diet, but I don't care. Show me how you can fuck me without fucking me."

"Spread your legs." He did so, and I placed my cock between those beautiful golden thighs, hard up against his balls. "Now close your legs. Just as tight as you can!"

I felt my cock being gripped tightly in the orifice formed by his thighs and his scrotum. With my thighs straddling his, I forced his legs even more tightly together. I could feel his hard, throbbing cock pressed against my belly. He clung to me as I kissed him, and we rocked and moaned until we both soared to a shrieking climax as I exploded between his lovely thighs and he shot off against my belly. For a long moment we lay there, still pressed against each other, not wanting to break the spell.

"Oh, wow!" he said finally. "That was sensational! Can I do that to you, too?"

"Maybe some day, perhaps. For the time being, we'll do things my way, including a good spanking whenever I think you need one. Next time we do it this way, though, I'll show you how well it also works with you lying on your stomach."

He threw back the covers and got out of bed. "Now I'm all sticky. Do you mind if I grab another shower?"

"Be my guest."

"Do we have to sleep in that mess you just shot all over the sheets?"

"No, kid," I said wearily. "We can sleep in the other bedroom. Tomorrow you can change the sheets."

"What do you mean, ME change the sheets? You mean you don't have a sheet-changing slave? Or at least a cleaning lady?"

"Not on weekends. Besides, you're supposed to start your slave training tomorrow, so YOU will change the sheets."

"Okay," he said, "but I don't do windows!"

While he showered, I went into the kitchen and set up the coffee pot on its timer for next morning. He's so much like his father, I thought. God, I just couldn't go through it a second time around! Not counting affairs in between, and my five years with Alistair, who is now living in Houston, Texas, with his new pretty-boy. Will Jerry-Boy also grow up to hate poetry and music and make a million dollars?

We slept until eleven, when the bubbling of the coffee pot awakened us. I found myself lying in Jerry-Boy's embrace, those strong young golden-smooth arms clasping me tightly. He kissed me into full consciousness, his tongue probing my mouth.

"Not in the morning," I warned him. "Not unless you want to die a horrible death. Only boys your age can wake up in the morning kissing. Men my age have to brush their teeth first." His breath was just like his father's, as was his delicate body-scent.

"Do you remember what day this is, Jerry-Sir?" he asked.

"Unless we've slept around the clock, I believe it's Saturday."

"Today's the day I start my slave training, remember?"

I shoved him out of bed with my foot. He fell on the floor with a startled expression. "You just started it, asshole. Fetch our coffee. Right now!"

I have trained many slave boys in my career, and still I get let in for some surprises. Some delightful surprises!

To my amazement, Jerry-Boy took to it like the proverbial duck to water. For a spoiled, somewhat arrogant little J.A.P. who had been waited on by servants all of his life, he was gloriously and insatiably submissive! Several times I had to stop what I was doing to him because his thick, rigid cock stood out like a turnstile at the Canadian National Exhibition, and he was obviously too close to orgasm. I did not allow him to climax until we were ready to quit for the day, when I introduced him to a new delight: the buddy shower.

We had just finished our last piece of work, and I was relaxing in the recliner with Jerry-Boy sitting at my feet, his head resting on my lap as I stroked his curly hair. Natural ringlets, just like Socky.

"Did I please you, Sir?" he asked softly.

"So far," I grudgingly admitted. "You best keep up the good work, boy, if you know what's good for you."

"That shouldn't be any problem. Slavery comes very naturally if you've had a domineering Jewish mother."

"You're absolutely right," I agreed. "Jewish mothers and Catholic priests have given the world some truly great slaves! Now fetch us a couple of drinks. I'll have a martini, very dry, with a twist, and you may have whatever you wish."

"I'll just have a glass of dry sherry. I'm not a heavy drinker."

After he had brought our drinks and we were sipping them companionably, very comfortable in our new relationship, he asked,

"May I take a shower? I'm all sweaty and dirty from all the things we did today."

"No, you may not. *WE* will take a shower. I have some new things to show you."

"More sex education?"

"You got it, kid." I grabbed him by the hair and booted him toward the bathroom. He loved it.

When we entered the hot shower together, he came to me and wrapped himself in my arms and we kissed passionately under the hot, pounding stream. Then I gently moved him away from me and picked up the soap. Very slowly and sensuously, I soaped him from head to toe, pausing at his groin to wash his beautiful cock, then down to those lovely thighs. I turned him around facing the water and soaped his back, then those sweet melon-shaped buns, soaping in between the cheeks. With my cock pressed hard and throbbing against his anus, but being careful not to penetrate him, I gently massaged his dick until I felt him quiver and stiffen in the throes of sexual arousal. Then he fell back against me, leaning against me as I supported him with my left arm while I continued to beat him off with my right hand as he screamed in ecstasy under the hot shower. Unable to restrain himself, he leaned his head back and bit my neck as he ejaculated a hot, seemingly endless load.

"Oh, God! If you only knew what you do to me!" He turned to face me, crying and whimpering in my arms, then kissing me. With the never-tiring ardor and stamina of youth, he was already getting hard again. "Jerry-Sir, may I do the same thing with you?"

"Yes, of course. But I want you to use your hands differently. When you get through soaping me, I'll show you what to do."

He took what seemed forever to soap me all over, slowly, sensuously, as I had done to him. Finally he knelt in the shower and took my rigid cock in his mouth. "Please don't come," he said.

"Not in your mouth, Jerry-Boy. If I did, you'd rush out and spend the next six weeks at Mt. Sinai, having tests done."

He tongued me beautifully, excitingly, until I felt that a climax was imminent. Then I leaned up against the shower stall, under the water, with Jerry-Boy behind me. Gently I guided his left hand to my cock, his right hand to my ass. He did not flinch or pull away as he gently massaged my prostate with his finger while he beat me off with his other hand. Next thing it was I who was quivering and screaming in ecstasy, the slender boy behind me holding me in his arms, the boy who had just done so perfectly and so beautifully what his very own father had taught me so long ago. I smiled tolerantly as he washed his right hand vigorously to remove any taint.

We stepped out of the shower and I stood commandingly, like Caesar, as he took thick towels from the rack and carefully, gently, thoroughly dried me off. When he knelt at my feet to dry them, he very deliberately raised each one in turn to his mouth and kissed it. Then he clasped his arms around my knees and ran his lips all over me, every part of me that he could reach. There was slave-worship and adoration in every fiber of his being as we returned to the living-room for another round of drinks.

"As soon as you've finished your drink," I ordered him, "you'll get your worthless butt into the kitchen and fix dinner. You'll find everything you need."

"But I've never fixed anything in my life except peanut butter sandwiches!" he exclaimed in dismay. "At home we have a cook! Even Gertrude and Al don't cook any more."

"I'm sure they're probably too busy with their Hadassah and B'nai B'rith, right?"

"And Israel Bonds. They're very active."

"All right, then, you useless klutz. You will memorize three chapters of *The Leatherman's Handbook* while I fix dinner!"

But he had, after all, been so very good. When he had set the table – at least he was able to do that! – and I had brought in a platter of cornish game hens garnished with vegetables, as well as rice pilaf, hot rolls, and a salad, I stopped him as he was about to kneel at my feet.

"In the bottom drawer of the large dresser you'll find a black lacquer box. Fetch it."

"Yes, Jerry-Sir."

Inside was a beautiful studded black leather collar that I had bought once upon a time in San Francisco. It had waited for many years for the right slave boy. I could think of no one in the world more appropriate than Socky's offspring.

Once again he knelt at my feet, and I buckled the collar around his lovely neck. "Wear it with pride, and make sure you always deserve it," I admonished him. "Now pour the wine."

After dinner we lay in front of the fireplace, the boy's head resting in my lap just as Socky had lain so many years before. I almost wanted to play Tchaikowsky's *Pathetique* on the stereo but did not dare; I would not have been able to handle it, so I played some Brahms and Berlioz instead. We went to bed, eventually, while it was still early. The weather was still brutal, and I teasingly asked Jerry-Boy if he wouldn't rather continue his street boy fantasy out on Yonge Street.

As it turned out, there were several other things we did that night that he much preferred to fantasy, as I showed him some more exciting techniques of germ-free sex. We slept, finally, clasped together like long-time lovers.

Sunday morning was mild and sunny. We took the Bloor Street subway out to High Park and walked the entire length of the park, down to the frozen lakefront. We frolicked in the snow, threw snowballs at each other and generally behaved like a couple of kids in love.

When we got home, we drank hot chocolate and ate a quick brunch. Then we got dressed for the beer bust at the Leather Corral. I was a little apprehensive.

"Jerry-Boy," I warned him, "you know by now that in our scene, a master is known by the slaves he keeps. If you do anything to embarrass or humiliate me in front of my brothers . . . ."

He looked hurt. "I promise you I won't. No more smart-ass J.A.P. spouting big words."

And indeed, he acquitted himself in a totally exemplary manner. When I led him into the leather bar on his leash, wearing his new studded collar and a leather harness, there were oohs and aahs of admiration. All in all, it turned out to be a very pleasant afternoon, with rounds and pitchers of beer flowing back and forth. Naturally, Jerry-Boy was seldom addressed directly; mostly they asked me, "What's his name?" or "Where did you acquire him?" But when spoken to directly, he answered briefly and politely, and always with a respectful "Sir." I was really amazed at how much he had absorbed so quickly. After we got back to my apartment and changed out of leather, I rewarded him by taking him out to an excellent dinner at my favorite Hungarian restaurant, where we drank three whole bottles of Egri Bikaver and even paid the strolling gypsies to play for us.

That night he clung to me closer than ever.

"Why can't I stay with you forever and ever?" he demanded to know.

"Don't tell me," I replied. "You have this adolescent fantasy about eternal romance. Hand in hand into the sunset, and all that sort of thing."

He was justifiably crushed. "All that sort of thing, eh? Like this morning in High Park? Was that just that sort of thing?"

"No," I admitted. "I'll remember this morning all my life. This whole weekend, in fact."

"I'm very serious, Jerry-Sir! This is not a fantasy! This is the real thing! Look, we're hot sex together. We both don't smoke, except pot. We both play chess. We both read books. We both like to wake up to Mozart in the morning. Why can't you recognize perfection when it hits you on the head?"

"Because it isn't perfect. For one thing, we're a whole generation apart. Besides, I'm a firm believer in long engagements. Look, you're still very young. You can't possibly know at this point where your head is."

"I'm a Capricorn," he pointed out. "When I make up my mind, nothing ever changes it."

"And I'm a Gemini. I might find a hot young trick on Yonge Street tomorrow night and forget you ever existed." I should have bitten off my tongue. He broke loose from me and lay on the other side of the bed. In a moment I heard him crying. I took him in my arms.

"That was a rotten thing to say," I said, kissing his tears. "I apologize. I know I'll never again meet anyone like you."

Just as I'd never again met anyone like Socky, who now hated poetry and had made a million dollars. Until this weekend, that is. Was there some sort of genetic magic that made Jerry-Boy appeal to me in the same way that his father had?

"Please," he pleaded. "Let me stay."

"No, Jerry-Boy. In the morning you go home. What are you going to tell your parents?"

"No problem. Gertrude and Al are used to me hanging out all weekend."

"You really do need some discipline."

"You see? That's another good reason you should make me stay with you." He wiped his eyes and blew his nose. "I'll tell you one thing, though. You can kick me out in the morning, but you haven't seen the last of me. I promise you that."

"Want to bet?" I answered cruelly.

Monday morning we drank our coffee and then walked to the Wellesley Street subway station. He went north, I went south. From the opposite platforms we waved goodbye to each other as our trains pulled in. I think I really intended never to see him again.

All morning I sat at my desk at Boredom, Bullcrap and Bad Grammar, Ltd., purveyors of advertising and public relations and other putrid forms of hype. Outside my window the sky had darkened again, and snow was falling. The aftermath of my enchanted weekend was a pall of depression that matched the winter skies.

What in the hell am I doing here? I asked myself. I should be in the States, where the booze is so much cheaper and the gay life a lot more fun. I should be in warm, sunny Florida, which in winter becomes Canada's eleventh province as the motels run up the Canadian flag along with their winter rates.

By noon I couldn't stand it any longer. I stormed into my boss's office and told him I was going stark, raving mad, and unless I could have a few weeks in the hot sun I was going to jump off a tall building. After some discussion of the client workload, he told me to go ahead – the leave of absence, that is, not the tall building.

I spent the rest of the week getting all my work caught up. In the evenings I dined out with friends or went to artsy little out-of-the-way theaters. I didn't want to hear the phone ring. A couple of times Jerry-Boy did call, but I refused to see him. Finally, on Friday night I told him I was leaving town for a few weeks. I wouldn't tell him where.

"Jerry-Sir, this is ridiculous! Can't we spend one last evening together?"

"I think it's better that we don't," I replied. But what I thought about that night as I lay in bed alone was how I had broken up with his father thirty years earlier.

My family had moved to California, and although I was out of high school and a free agent, I had opted to go with them. New places, travel, adventure – the lure was too great to resist. Socky had stayed to go to college. We pledged eternal devotion and really meant it, too. At first we wrote every day, then every week. Finally he wrote that he had met someone else. Just for sex and good company, of course; he knew I'd understand. The someone else became a succession of someone elses; then, finally, bowing to family pressure, he'd married Gertrude.

No more love. No more poetry. No more Tchaikowsky's *Pathetique.* But he'd made a million dollars, and he'd had Jerry-Boy, who was so much like young Socky that he had me running scared. My bags were all packed, the car all serviced and ready to go. I ran, and I didn't look back.

There is absolutely nothing better than a long driving trip to clear one's head of excess baggage. I stopped along the way to visit relatives, look up old friends, and sample the local watering holes. By the time I finally arrived in Fort Lauderdale a week later, I had put the entire bizarre episode out of my mind. Well, almost.

It was good to be back in South Florida. I partied, I got drunk, I smoked lots of good dope, I hit all the leather bars and discos. I partied. I ate too much and started to gain weight. I partied. I spent my days on the beach and at night I partied. Of course I never thought about Jerry-Boy once.

I thought about him constantly.

It was on my seventh day in Fort Lauderdale that I was lying on the beach across from the Marlin, surrounded by hundreds of beautiful gay bodies and a few old leather dudes. I had my eyes closed, soaking up the delicious Florida sun and thinking about the snow and ice back home. Vaguely I was aware of someone lying down next to me, but I didn't pay any attention until a shockingly familiar voice said,

"May I borrow your sunscreen, please?"

"Oh, no," I groaned, and opened my eyes. There he was, stretched out beside me, propped on one elbow, looking more enchanting than ever. He looked exactly as Socky had looked during those idyllic summers at our families' adjacent cottages on Georgian Bay. I ran the gamut of mixed emotions, but mainly I wanted to grab him and make love to him. Instead I said;

"What's a nice Jewish boy from Toronto doing in a place like this?"

"I followed you down here." He flashed his bright, serendipitous smile. "See, I had this fantasy about Blondel chasing after King Richard the Lion Heart all over Europe, strumming his lute and every stray cock he happened to latch onto."

"So you just came strumming along. What about home and school?"

"I cut a deal with my dad. Gertrude and Al gave me a long paid vacation in Fort Lauderdale provided I return to school for spring term, and take at least one business course."

"Sounds fair to me. How did you know where I was?"

"You'd really make a lousy spy, you know. Rub some of this on my back, would you please? Your boss didn't mind telling me you were on your way to Fort Lauderdale. Neither did your building superintendant. So here I am!"

"But what if I hadn't been staying at the Marlin? This is the busy season, you know."

"Then I'd have called all the other gay guest houses and motels. I bought a gay guide on Yonge Street before I left."

"What if I'd been staying with friends?"

"Then I'd have called the bike clubs and the gay organizations. I'd have found you somehow."

"All right, Jerry-Boy, you win for now. Where, or with whom, are you staying?"

"With you, of course. I just got off the plane."

"Okay," I sighed resignedly. "Have your luggage brought up to my room. Our room."

"I already have."

"You WHAT?"

"Oh don't get upset. They wouldn't let me into your room, of course, but I convinced them to let me drop off my luggage. So all I have to do is unpack. Will you take me to a leather bar tonight?"

"After I tie you up and spank the hell out of you."

"You had to say that. Now look what you just did!"

Indeed, he could barely keep it concealed inside his Speedo.

I think those weeks in Fort Lauderdale were the most idyllic I had ever experienced. For one thing, Jerry-Boy never ran out of fantasies. One night it was disco fanstasy, next night it was gourmet cuisine fantasy. We both got golden tans and made love frequently in the shower and in bed. Safely and hygienically, of course.

It was our most exotic sexual fantasy of all that turned out to be the climax, if I may be forgiven the double entendre, of the whole affair. One night, after we had just made love, Jerry-Boy whispered into my ear,

"I want a very special favor from you."

"Can I afford it?"

"This won't cost you anything at all. At least, not in money."

"Okay, let's hear it, kid."

"Tomorrow night," he said dreamily, "I call the shots. We do everything my way."

I thought about it for a moment. "That's kind of a biggie."

"Come on," he persisted. "As close as we've become, I don't see where it's unreasonable." His hand was playing with my cock as he licked my ear. "Please. Just trust me, okay?"

"Oh, all right," I agreed, not without feeling a thrill of anticipation. "I guess you've earned it."

I returned home the following evening after a day of literary research at the beautiful new Fort Lauderdale public library. As I entered our room, it was dark, with the aroma of incense and pot in the air. "Jerry-Boy?" I called out.

Suddenly I heard the crack of my own cat-o'-nine-tails and felt the lash of leather across my back. From out of the gloom came Jerry-Boy's voice, hard as steel.

"Get on your knees, asshole."

"Hey! Come on, now, Jerry-Boy! Knock it off!"

Another stinging lash of leather across my back. Now he stepped out into the light, wearing his own brand new harness and chaps. Brand new black leather boots, too.

"Nice gear, kid." Actually, he was absolutely gorgeous! He looked very much the leather-magazine fantasy of a hot young leather top-man stepping out of its pages.

"I couldn't very well use *your* chaps," he said. "My God, how did you ever get them made without the cow becoming an endangered species?"

"You little wimp!" I exclaimed. "I'm going to punish you very severely for that!"

"Not tonight you're not," he replied. "Remember, I call all the shots tonight! Now, just shut up and sit down and I'll tell you all about this great fantasy I've been thinking about the past few days."

I mixed us a couple of drinks and it all came pouring out. "I want to play Daddy!" he explained. "I keep having this fantasy about picking you up in my arms! I want to carry you around the room impaled on my cock! I want to do everything with you that you can do with me!"

"Jerry-Boy," I said, "there are certain immutable, irrevocable laws of physics. I weigh two hundred pounds. You weigh about 145 soaking wet. I suppose I could call up Cape Canaveral and ask if we could go along on the next space shuttle. I've heard that in a weightless environment any sexual position is feasible."

"It doesn't have to be aboard a space shuttle. We can do it in the water, too. We'll go to the tubs!"

"The tubs? What about your paranoid obsession with hygienic, germ-free sex?"

"I'd hardly call it paranoid, these days. We'll use a rubber, just as we've been doing. And anyway, it won't be a problem any more once we're married."

"Once we're WHAT?"

"They do have a gay synagogue here, don't they?"

"Well, of course. In South Florida how could they not have? It's called Congregation Etz-Chaim. But Jerry-Boy, aside from the fact that I've never said we were playing for keeps, I'm not the slightest bit religious! I don't believe in formal marriage. It's so — well, so unliberated."

"I don't care. I've always had this fantasy about having a big Jewish wedding."

"What are you going to do, wear a bridal dress and stand under the canopy and break the wine glass?"

"Not a bridal dress. Leather will do, and I'll settle for whatever ceremony of formal commitment to each other they do in a gay *schul*. Oh, I realize it's not legally binding, but that's not important to us! Just think about it. I'm not pushing, you understand.

I've already made up my mind. You just think about it. That's all I ask. Maybe after tonight you'll be ready to make your decision."

So off we went to the baths, where I rented their largest V.I.P. double room. We'd brought along a bottle of iced champagne, and we drank a couple of glasses apiece as we enjoyed preliminary lovemaking in our room. Finally Jerry-Boy said, "I'm ready now."

He slipped a rubber onto that gigantic boy-cock of his and then wrapped his towel around himself. "I'll race you to the pool!" he said. "Last one in's a disco twinkie!"

We ran out to the pool and dove in. Fortunately, it was heated, because the night air was rather cool, for South Florida, that is. Also fortunately, it was mid-week, and not crowded. There was no one else in the pool area as Jerry-Boy began to enact his fantasy.

With his arms around me, he led me into neck-deep water, and then, in the buoyancy of the warm pool, he lifted me into his arms as easily as I had carried him into the bedroom on our very first night. I clung to him as he kissed me long and hard.

"Can you float on your back?" he asked.

"Sure," I said. He had already greased my ass liberally. I lay back upon the water, floating peacefully under the stars.

Jerry-Boy spread my legs apart. Although I'd fucked him with a rubber several times, he'd never fucked me. Even if I'd been willing to let him, he was still hung-up about getting a germ on his penis. But this time, he gently but firmly inserted that gigantic boy-cock. I almost screamed, not from the slight pain at first, but from the sublime ecstasy as I felt the mass of it penetrate me to the hilt.

"Wrap your legs around me real tight, the way I do when you fuck me in this position. Yeah, man, that's it! Now wrap your arms around my neck the way I do when you carry me around on your cock."

I felt his strong young arms behind me, clasping me, clasping me by the cheeks of my ass, forcing himself into me to the very limit as I clung to him. At that moment the champagne and the pot kicked in real hard, and in a weird flash of mind-link I felt as though the boy had entered my own memory-fantasy. Suddenly I was sixteen years old again, and Socky and I were making love in the boat-house of his parents' summer cottage. Then, under a clear and starry sky, we splashed and frolicked naked in the ice-cold waters of that northern lake.

We were kissing long and hard while he fucked me in the sensuous warmth of the water. Finally, Jerry-Boy said, "How do you feel – right now?"

My whole *persona* was gone, transfigured from a burly, grizzled old leather dude into a whimpering teenage boy being carried about impaled on his young lover's huge cock.

"I feel . . . . " I could barely whisper into his ear. "I feel as though I totally belong to you."

"You do. You always have." He was talking very low and sexily into my ear. "You have from that very first night. You might as well get used to it. I own you. I possess you. You belong to me just as much as I belong to you." His hips were keeping up a steady rhythm, pounding me to the ultimate climax. "You are mine. Now and forever. You are mine. My cock in your ass. My juice and my love inside of you. God! Jerry-Sir! Hang onto me! Hang onto me! Now!" He planted his lips firmly on my own and I felt his enormous boy-cock ejaculate great spurts of his love inside the rubber. Thank goodness it didn't break, or he'd probably have run screaming to Mt. Sinai and checked in for six weeks of tests.

Back at the Marlin, we drank another bottle of champagne in our room. Then I lay back in his arms. He was very much the young leather top that evening.

"So," he said. "I think we have what the lawyers call a meeting of the minds."

"But we don't" I protested. "I haven't agreed to anything!"

He went on, undismayed. "We'll get married in Etz-Chaim, between the services and the *Oneg Shabbat.*"

"It's a lovely fantasy, Jerry-Boy, but what happens when we go home?"

"What do you mean, what happens? You have that fantastic apartment for us to live in. We can even install a big hot-tub."

"Look, kid," I pointed out, "Alistair's paid-up lease runs out very soon. Do you have any idea what that penthouse suite costs?"

"I'd guess around fifteen hundred a month. See, I wasn't brought up in the real estate business for nothing."

"So what are you going to do? Have your father buy the building and then rent us the apartment for four hundred a month? Are you going to tell him you're living with a lover, who just happens to be someone he knew in high school?"

"He doesn't ever have to know that. See, Gertrude and Al don't really care where I'm living as long as I keep in touch and stay healthy. As for the rent, I have a little income of my own from a trust fund my Aunt Esther left me, she should rest in peace. That, plus your work and your writing, we'll make out okay. Just trust me."

"You crazy kid! I'm over twice your age, and you tell me to trust you! I'm not even sure I want a permanent relationship!"

"Of course you do. You know that's where it's at. Please."

"The answer is no. And stop playing with my cock."

"You want me to use the whip on you again, Sir?"

"I want you to quit making me horny. How can a man think clearly when he's horny?"

"You want to go through the rest of your life and never again have sex the way we did in that pool tonight? But always, always remembering it?"

"Oh, God! You should be selling real estate like your father. You come up with such great closing arguments. Leave my tits alone."

"Think of the long winter nights playing chess in front of the fireplace. You could even write your novel."

"I couldn't. We'd be too busy fucking."

"Would you ever cheat on me or trick out with someone else?"

"Of course not! Would I drink cheap wine when I have Dom Perignon at home? Jerry-Boy, I just don't know what to say."

"Then just say 'I love you.' Because I sure as hell love you!"

I thought about it for a long moment. I wanted to tell him, you'll grow up and break my heart, and at my age I don't need it. You'll learn to hate poetry and music, and make a million dollars. But damn it, I'm not about to go through the rest of my life with my seat belt fastened! Why the hell did you have to be Socky's kid?

But all I said was, "All right, kid. We'll give it a try. We can even do that stupid thing in the synagogue. But after that, let's pack up and head home. I'm tired of paradise. I need to get back to work, even though it'll still be winter up there."

"No, it won't. We can take it slow and easy and party our way up the coast. We'll stop in all the big cities and check out the leather bars and discos. We'll spend nights in funky little motels and truck stops. I have this fantasy where you're a truck driver and I'm a college kid hitch-hiking. By the time we get home, it'll be spring."

"Do you have any more fantasies I should be aware of?"

"Yes," he said, that beautiful boyish smile on his face. He was lying naked on the bed, the soft light highlighting his slender beauty. "I've always had this fantasy about taking a long honeymoon trip with my new lover. Have you noticed how my fantasies have a way of turning into realities?"

"I had a fantasy once," I said.

"And what happened?"

"I had to wait thirty long years. But it finally became a reality."

Two Drink Knockout

FRANK MOSCA

Normally the two drinks that are my limit don't bother me, but this morning I woke because the ants were making too much noise. The pounding of their feet in the walls was driving me crazy.

I bleared at the clock so hard it looked beige instead of its normal white, and I admitted it: I had a hangover. Either that or I was dying, and right now that seemed preferable. What really disturbed me though was the good looking man beside me. He was about twenty-seven, dark haired, moustached, and built like he'd spent the last three years of his life in a gym.

His name was Andy. I vaguely remembered meeting him at the bar, but that was all. I didn't even remember asking him home. That scared me, too. Hell, I knew the stats about people running around with herpes, or worse, so I'd been real careful. I don't mean paranoid or celibate, just careful. I rolled out of bed, fell actually, aimed for the head, and walked into a wall.

"Ah, Tom," Andy mumbled quietly, "Bathroom's that way." He pointed.

I looked around. I wasn't even at my own apartment.

Andy glanced up as I returned and smiled wryly. "You look like hell," he said, "but I still think you're sexy."

I groaned and collapsed back onto the bed.

He rolled over to look at me. "To set your mind at rest, if it's functioning at the moment, no we didn't have a mad passionate night of sex and fun, though I don't mind that at all. But as horny as I was when I undressed you and rolled you into bed, I wasn't about to let my gonads get the better of me. I didn't think it'd be kosher. I felt it'd only be fair to both of us if I asked you if there was any reason we shouldn't – medical or otherwise. I admit it, I enjoy being healthy. I've got lots of plans for the next few decades and I want to stick around to accomplish them." He yawned and stretched. "But believe me, that doesn't mean I'm upset about having you here.

"I'd seen you at the bar twice before but I've never had the guts to come over and meet you. That's why I was really thrilled last night when you stopped and asked me to dance, then sat and talked for about forty minutes."

I tried to sit up but laid back down. The world was still spinning, though not so much as before. I didn't remember any of that.

Andy stifled a smile and continued. "Then you ordered another Screaming Orgasm and nearly passed out at the table. Normally, I'd just leave someone like that, but you seemed nice and even the waiter was amazed. He claimed he'd never even seen you tipsy. So I decided to get you home and to bed to keep you from getting hurt."

I could feel myself blushing. "I usually drink Kahlua and creams. I've never had a Screaming Orgasm before but one of my friends raved so much about how good they were I figured I'd try a few. I didn't realize they were so strong. I guess I don't have much alcohol tolerance."

He eyed me quizzically. "Want a couple of aspirin?"

I groaned a yes and he padded away to the medicine chest. Even through the hangover I couldn't help but notice the smoothness of his movement. He was like a cat, lean and lithe. I felt my cock start to respond. By the time he was back, the tent under the covers was obvious. My attempted grin felt more like a grimace.

"It's your fault, and to answer your previous question, I'm unattached and as healthy as one man can be with pounding that threatens to rip its way through my skull."

He handed me the pills and a glass of water. Then he slipped his head under the covers as I swallowed the aspirin. I felt his tongue run up the shaft and across my balls. I groaned – only partly from the hangover. He popped out from under the sheets and gave me a kiss.

"The idea appeals to me," he said, "but I work on Saturdays and I've got to get ready. You're welcome to stay. All day if you'd like, after all if you can't trust a county probation officer, who can you trust?"

I gasped. "I told you that?" I never told that to anyone I didn't know well.

He nodded. "If you prefer, the information stops here." He rolled out of bed. "I'll be home by six and we can have supper.

"By the way, if you decide you'd rather leave, your car's downstairs. The doorman at the bar happened to notice where you parked so I had a friend drive it over for you last night." He smiled and turned for the bathroom.

"Andy," I said softly. He turned back. "Thank you for this." I pointed to the bed. "I'll also take you up on your offer, but only if you let me treat."

"Okay. Get some rest."

I stuck my head under the pillow. I didn't even hear him leave. I woke again about three. My head throbbed a bit but a few more aspirin and a warm bath took care of that, then I puttered around the apartment. It'd been too long since I'd met anyone as considerate as Andy. Hell, some of the guys I knew would have left me with clap or worse without an afterthought. I was impressed, not only by that but by his bookcases too.

It seemed Andy wasn't only stunning, he was bright. His shelves overflowed with books on physics, philosophy, and three –ologies I wasn't even sure about, and I'm no dummy. Just when I began to think he was totally out of my league I found complete collections of Doonesbury and Andy Capp. I was into my third Doonesbury book when he got home. Thankfully, I'd dressed well when I'd gone out because he walked in with the most stunning brunette I'd ever seen in my life. She was tall as he and dressed so well that to say she looked like a model would be insulting.

"Tom. This is my sister, Jennifer. She stopped by to say hi."

"Oh, bull." Jennifer said lightly as she shook my hand. "The truth is Andy called me this afternoon to brag about you and I had to see what had him so hot and bothered. I met him downstairs and wouldn't let him talk me out of coming up."

"Jen!!" Andy yelped.

I stood there feeling slightly stupid and pleased all at once.

"He's right." She continued to me. "You are a great looking man." She smiled. "And I'm sure you're as nice a man as you are good looking. Andy's never been stupid. He told me you were and I quote, the most outstanding man he's met in his life, unquote."

I glanced at Andy. He was blushing furiously and looking as if he wanted to hide under a postage stamp. I was becoming more thrilled by the minute.

"But," she said, "I have to leave. I've got a date myself." She leaned close, kissed me, and whispered, "He's going to kill me later, but I had to. You wouldn't believe it to look at him, but he's shy. He'd never tell you all that himself."

"Jen," Andy demanded pointedly. "What time's that date?"

"I'm off. I know where the door is. Bye you two. Have fun."

Neither of us moved till we heard the door close. I glanced at Andy and he blushed again. We both exploded in laughter.

"I'm sorry . . . " he started finally.

"Don't be. I think she's great. I'm also sorry I don't have a sis like that. I have to tell you all by myself that I think you're hot."

He blushed again.

"My god!" My surprise was honest. "You really don't know how good looking you are."

He looked at me and I nodded. He came close. Our bodies locked in a kiss. I could feel his muscles, his warmth, and I wanted him badly. I looked into his eyes and I unbuttoned his shirt, and he mine. We kicked off our shoes and moved to the bedroom.

"Let me do that," I said as he fumbled with his belt. I loosened it, then playfully slid my tongue under his nipple. He groaned softly and I ran my hand over the bulge in his pants.

He nibbled my earlobe and drove me wild. In almost one motion, I shucked off my pants and his and we fell to the bed. I could feel drops of precome moistening my cock. Andy moved low and I felt his tongue moving over my groin, teasing, flicking, caressing. I arched off the bed as his tongue slid to my cock, wetting it. Almost immediately, he began a slow hand squeeze up my shaft, adding a half twist as he reached the top. I arched higher. His tongue flicked against my balls. It was too much. I came, squirting come through his fingers. I didn't go soft or relax, but pulled him to me, kissed him, and sought his cock.

I'd never been with an uncut man before. I loved it immediately. His cock was classically beautiful, his balls lightly covered with hair. Andy twitched gently, his breath coming in short gasps, as I traced my fingertips in a soft tattoo on his ball sack. Suddenly, he twisted slightly making sure he didn't lose contact with my hand and reached into his dresser drawer.

"I've got a present for you."

"Uh huh?" I slid my tongue where my fingertips had been and traced the outline of his balls. "Animal?" I lapped again. "Vegetable?" I nuzzled his thighs. "Or mineral?"

He sat up easily and buried his face in my hair. "All three, you lucky devil. Animal." He pointed to himself as he traced his tongue across my left ear. "Vegetable." He followed the hair line of my chest with a tube of KY. "And mineral." He tore open a small aluminum packet, and slid a condom onto my cock.

I glanced down and laughed so hard he had to hold me. The rubber had two eyes and a mouth printed on it. It looked like a giggling snake.

"Please, Tom. Fuck me first. I stayed awake over an hour last night thinking about you fucking me. I didn't even get much work done today thinking about it."

I moved between his legs. We kissed. I wanted him more than I've ever wanted anyone. I nuzzled his balls again. The aroma of his body brought me higher than I'd been till now. My hands roamed across his washboard stomach, then up to his pecs.

"That tickles, and it's cold even through the rubber." I told him as he laved KY onto my cock.

"It won't be." He pulled me close. "Please." He moaned. "Now. Please."

I entered him gently. We came together. His come splattered my chest and his stomach.

"Damn," he whispered softly.

"Yeah, damn." I rolled the rubber off, and lay beside him. He tangled his fingers in my hair then ran his hand slowly down the bridge of my nose. "Still think I'm quote, the most outstanding man you've ever met, unquote?" I teased.

He blushed, then held his hand out parallel. "So-so." There was a gleam in his eye.

I started to stand but he yanked me back onto the bed by my ankle. "Ah huh!" I yelped. "You do care."

"It's not that," he said lightly. "You promised to treat me tonight and I'm not letting you go till you do."

"Fine with me." I twisted suddenly, licking my finger, and teased under his foreskin. He squirmed and whimpered softly, then exploded in laughter and pushed me away.

"Stop," he gasped. "It tickles so good, it's killing me."

"Does that count as a treat?"

"Well . . . Did you really mean it last night, or was it just the alcohol, when you said you wanted my hard cock up your virgin ass?"

"What? Did I really say that?"

"Yes." He spoke solemnly while shaking his head no.

"I love it." I ran my hand slowly through the hair of his chest, then snuggled in his arms. "You're crazy."

"How did you guess?"

"Because I never use the word virgin to describe myself. Hunky – of course, charming – usually, articulate – always, modest – sometimes, but virgin – never." I fingered his foreskin idly and watched his cock start to rise. "Of course if I didn't ask, I should have. But only if you've got one of those cute rubbers. I want to see what they look like coming at me on that weapon of yours."

In answer he reached back, grabbed another packet, then entered me. I shook spasmodically as his thrusting massaged my prostate, and I clutched at his body. His thighs tensed, his breathing became shallower, his thrusting faster. He threw back his head and

I felt his cock expand. I came again. He started to withdraw.

"No, please, don't pull out yet," I begged. "I want to look at you for a minute."

He traced a pattern across my eyebrow with his right forefinger, then held out his hand in the so-so gesture and shook his head no. He shifted it to a thumbs up. He slid out of me and I pulled him to me. He bent and kissed me softly.

"You want to get something to eat?" he asked. "Or shall we stay here the rest of the night?"

"I'm starved. Let's just relax a minute, then we can get ready."

"What's the matter?" he joked. "No stamina?"

"It's not that, Andy." I searched his eyes. They were so dark they were almost black. "I've just got a hunch we'll have plenty of time for all the sex we want."

He returned my gaze thoughtfully. A half smile lighted his lips and he nodded slowly. "I think Jen is going to get a rose for opening her mouth."

"Make it two."

He did. This year she got four for our second anniversary.

Under Glass

DARRELL YATES RIST

Back home warm beside the reading lamp. My hands, red and chapped from a chill, wet, February weekend in Bermuda, glowed beneath the light like stop signs caked with splatter after road crews dump their salty loads in a snow storm. Three raw days chafing against the winter sea wind on a motor bike had been my compensation for missing out on St. Croix with my lover. "Bob and four hot men," I thought. "Eight days. Two nights with him for each of them – unless one of them gets lucky and gets a little more."

Bermuda hadn't been so full of possibilities. But I knew something of that before the trip – and thought it just as well. A friend, a friend who'd been a lover, had been taken to the hospital the day I left. With pneumonia, *the* pneumonia. From the airport as the plane was boarding, I called another friend whom I knew would want to know.

"All the better, then," he said, "you're going to Bermuda."

"*Any* place would do," I rattled fast (the boarding line had dwindled to the final two, neither one with carry-ons to argue over with the gate attendant, slow their pace). "Any place out of New York and away from gay diseases."

"That's exactly what I'm saying. In Bermuda you won't find much to make you think of sex."

"You've been there?" I rushed (*one* was left in line).

"No. I'm looking in this guide book. One gay bar in the whole place."

"What's it called?" I hurried him, pulling the cap off my Bic with my teeth.

"The Gazebo – in the Princess Hotel in Hamilton."

"Thanks. Gotta go."

"Wait." I heard him call as I was taking the receiver from my ear. "The book here says Bermudians aren't really *fond* of gays. We're illegal – *very*. Just thought you'd want to know," he sang, "in case you change your mind and go out cruising."

"Wonderful," I sneered. "Bye."

+ + + + + + + +

"That bar's closed," said the woman on the telephone. British rhythm and articulation, accent mid-American, the lush commixture beautifully Bermudian, but with enough insulted haughtiness to suggest that I not press my query further. And finding nothing under "Gay" but last names in the phone book, I rode my rented moped through a chilly rain to Hamilton to look for clues – the kind that loiter, lonely and half hidden, like degenerates surviving a watchful hatred that would prefer them dead: bookstores selling porn, if only straight, where men might signal other men with slow and cautious eyes, faint beacons in the North Atlantic fog; dark paths through bushes in a park; or heavy shadows in abandoned buildings by the wharf. But I found nothing with the vaguest scent of homosexuality and, having scavenged for an hour in the cold on my bike, I turned towards a bookstore, *legitimate*, I remembered from my last trip to Bermuda 15 years before.

I was sailing then: a sleek, black sloop, *Black Fox, manned* with a crew of four. I was only 22. The skipper – with his thick, sun-bleached hair and pale blue eyes, his strong, slender body charred brown and shaped by years of hoisting sails, heaving in lines, steadying the wheel in heavy seas – was somewhere in his early 30s, mature and rugged, everything I thought a man should be. He'd lie nude on deck on days when the wind and skies were good in the Caribbean, the narrow swatch of hair down his stomach – from the middle of his chest to his crotch – bristling gold, a glistening pathway to the shaft of dark brown flesh which hung thick and lazy between his legs with its foreskin gathered to a gentle point, an arrow to his ass. On my mid-day watch, I'd stare. I'd never seen a man whose nakedness was so comfortable, so natural. I'd never had a man. And I'd wait, stunned by the tropic heat and my desire, for the faintest stirring of his cock as though it were the potent needle of a compass commanding me to pleasures I had never known.

It was he who took me to the bookshop 15 years ago. In a biting mist, we'd ridden from St. Georges, where the boat was docked, to Hamilton, half way across Bermuda, to buy Sir Francis Chichester's *The Clipper Way*. As I read the book, I put him and me in every one of the salty stories of men cloistering for months in tiny yachts – with crews sometimes of only two and the palest thoughts of even meager privacy foresworn – to circumnavigate the earth like the sailors in the clipper ships. One night when we were drinking at the White Horse Pub by the harbor in St. Georges, he'd slap me on the back or squeeze his arm around my shoulder roughly every now and then to punctuate something that he'd said. Such intimacy to him, I guess, was simply genial. Or paternal: he'd taught me everything I knew about the open sea. But his gruff caresses fed my fantasies. I watched the flames from the pub's stone hearth flicker in his eyes, orange searing blue like a fiery sunset. He began to talk about how horny sailors get at sea: "nothing but your hand," he laughed, "or rubbing on the sheets." I felt my skin enflame, redden like the embers in the fireplace at my back. I couldn't speak – just drank, looking out the window by the water, hoping I'd come off thoughtful, lost in manly revery. "Did I ever tell you how I want to die?" he asked suddenly. I looked up startled at the change. He held his beer in front of his face, watched the frenzied colors of the fireplace melting through the mug. "When I'm, say, 35, still at my prime, going down on some sweet sixteen-year old," he said, leaning over the table confidentially. "Pumping a nice, young pussy, and just as I explode and fill her hole, my heart goes 'pop!'"

Back in the bookshop this trip to Bermuda, I looked for *The Clipper Way* again, for a reminiscing reread. And scanning the shelves for "Chichester," I rubbed my cock through the pocket of my pants, feeling it grow warm and full as I thought of the handsome sailor who for all I knew might well have died years ago, his heart blowing apart while he fucked a teenage cunt. The book was out of stock.

+ + + + + + +

I'd already gotten the moped revved again for the ride back to my room before I noticed the small, square building sitting shadowed down a narrow path from the parking space. The rain had stopped, and a beam of brilliant sunshine now had broken through the clouds as though a prurient, heavenly lighting tech, on cue, had thrown a spot: the sign above the door read "Men."

No one was inside. I went from stall to stall to find grafitti. None. I went to a urinal and peed. Before I'd tucked my cock back in, the door opened slowly, as though timidly. For a minute, it was quiet. Then a tall, young man stepped up to the mirror. I could see him combing his hair, now and then looking over at me but quickly staring straight ahead if I turned my eyes his way. I moved back, just enough for him to see my cock next time he looked. I stroked it, held it out, long and hard, for him to see. He moved back too, now bold enough not to avert his eyes. He ran his hand slowly up and down his fly, then unzipped and loosed his prick. It stuck straight out, the foreskin covering half the head, gleaming red and wet. He cupped his hand, running it beneath the shaft, teasing. He moved up to a urinal. I moved over to the urinal next to him, and taking his cock in my hand, squeezed warm, clear liquid from his hole until it ran out thick in a long, unbroken strand like syrup. I caught it on my fingers and lubed myself. We both turned and arched our backs like bows, pointed our cocks toward one another and caressed them, slowly stroking their lengths.

I wanted to tongue the taut, smooth head of his shaft, taste the pungent moisture caught below the foreskin. Bending over to take him in my mouth, I stretched my tongue to lap the wet, heavy bead shining at the hole of his prick. Outside there were footsteps. The door creaked, opening, then creaked closed again. We shifted quickly, feigning the tremors at the end of a piss and ritually shaking our cocks. The door now opened again, and an old man shuffled in and lazily to a stall.

"Do you have a place?" the man beside me, clipped and British, whispered, trying so hard to speak beneath his breath he nearly choked.

"At Elbow Beach – the hotel."

"I'll meet you at the entry gate."

"It's a ways from here. You know where it is?"

"Oh yes." He was still adjusting, not quite zipped back up. I was at the door.

I handed him a card that had my name and told him the number of my room. "See you in a bit," I said. "Oh . . . and what's your name?"

He said nothing for a moment, still fidgeting with his shirttail and his pants. Then, "*James,*" he answered hastily, as though seizing something evanescent from the air. "You go ahead. I'll follow when you've gotten clear."

I waited for some 30 minutes at the hotel gate, another 30 in my room. He never came.

I had dinner, napped, and a little after 10:00 I tried again, mopedding back to Hamilton against a steady, shivering wind and drizzle. The town was almost empty. The public john was locked. I waited under an overhang, hoping that the rain would stop. From the corner pub a phrase or two of disco sometimes rolled into the street, a loud and pulsing surf, and ghostly figures, frosty in the light reflected from the sign above the door, appeared and disappeared like mists.

Near midnight, one man left the pub and started up the street toward me, every several paces stopping, as though to light, relight, a cigarette or catch himself. In the dense air, I couldn't tell. When he got abreast of me, he stepped beneath the eaves and let himself fall back against the wall.

"A drop too much to drink, mate," he said, slurring his brogue. He shut his eyes, then opening them quickly, sprang his head toward me. "And what you doin' out in the rain – and standin' here alone." His breath was sharp.

"Thinking of riding home," I said, looking hard into his eyes.

He wasn't what I might have wished, like brackish water fine for the forehead but only a tease to the thirst. But I liked his coarse blond hair and the weathered youth in his cheeks, a ruddy face that might have been a seaman's.

"And which way is that?" he asked brightly, as though he'd suddenly sobered.

"Just around the bay."

"That's my way too. But my mates went home without me. That your bike?" He pointed toward the street.

I nodded. He'd already started walking to the curb.

I had to ram the pedal several times to get the motor going. "So *this* is the cruisey place." I said as I mounted the bike.

"*This*? Not this. You won't find a place to cruise in Hamilton. Nowhere in Bermuda." He climbed on behind me and wrapped his arms around my waist. "Whatever you find here is just by chance, my friend. And as for the loo – once in your life you'd find another one in there." As we took off, he put his hands deep inside my pockets and pushed them down between my legs, warming my cock and balls with his fingers.

When we got into the hotel room, I went to pee. I peeled my shirt off pissing, splattering the floor and wall – I didn't care. And I stumbled to the bedroom pulling off my shoes and socks and pants. He – "Brian," he told me, with a vigorous trill on the *r* – was lying on the bed, his shirt off, his pants down to his knees. His chest was wide and smooth, his hairless stomach flat and snugly narrowed at the waist. Below his navel lay a plain of reddish yellow hair, which bushed, tangled and luxuriant, at his crotch. I reached down to lift his cock, soft and arching, the head a heavy pendulum fallen to the bed. Gently, I stretched out the shaft to feel its weight on my palm. His balls hung long and loose. Then lying on the bed, I put my face down on his thigh, held his cock and balls together near my mouth and with my other hand jerked off. He didn't move. He'd collapsed into a drunken sleep before I'd finished pissing when we first came in.

Next morning I woke early, showered, and got dressed. Then I waked him. While he took a piss, I called his cab.

\+ + + + + + +

The plane was late, the traffic into Newark stalling in a snow, and by the time the airport bus got to the Port Authority, it was close to midnight, some ten hours after checking out of my hotel. I'd finished *God's Bullies*, a saga of the homophobic politics of the New Religious Right, which I'd begun the night before (I didn't bother prowling on the second night). At home, after listening to the phone machine – my friend with AIDS wasn't doing any better – I thumbed the book, distracted, wishing there were more to read, intriguing stories which I'd not yet finished, which would rein my restlessness and keep me in.

I read the passages again on Terry Dolan. Young and handsome (I'd seen his picture in the paper many times) with a packaged, neat virility that's a code for homosexual. Powerful and ruthless: few among the ruling, right wing ideologues whose vision of America is anti-gay wield such a deadly will as he. One night, the story goes, a man named Richard (who tells all) met Dolan at the Eagle in D.C., went home and tricked with him. Only in the small talk after sex (one's honesty is often then unguarded, its defenses smoldering, flickering remnants of erotic conflagration), did Richard find out who his bedmate was.

Reading this again, I remembered years ago lying in the early morning moonlight on a park bench by the beach in Waikiki. Beside me knelt a man whom I'd just met. He'd been standing for a long time by a palm, talking to himself and clinging to his chest a large, black book. The brilliant moon was glinting off his hair, blonde but nearly white, bathing him – his naked chest and arms – in silver, a surfer's body caught beneath a breaking wave of light. I watched him for a while, then walked up to him and asked him if he'd let me suck his cock. He looked at me with tortured eyes and said that Jesus loved me and would exorcise the demon in my heart. He laid me down, got onto his knees, and opened up his Bible, its floppy covers winging like a raven just above my face. As he prayed for me – his voice was choked and trembling – I beat off.

This memory, like a photograph glimpsed unexpectedly among obscure mementos, called up shapeless fantasies and longing. I closed my book, walked over to the window, wondered where I'd go if I went out. The wind was writhing in the street, twisting through the snow in icy colonnades of glitter. In the apartment across the way, a man stood naked, stared at me. I'd beaten off many times for him before: in the window, I'd stripped off my clothes, massaged my body, slowly turning in a narrow beam of light directed from the floor. He'd dim his lights, stand frozen in the pallid glow, and as though mesmerized, do nothing more than watch until I'd lay my cock, tense and aching, up against the window pane, pull my balls back toward my ass, sharp, and with that, shoot, scalloping the glass with hot frosting. Then the room in which he stood would suddenly go black.

Tonight, I unbuttoned my jeans. My cock fell out, heavy, swelling with anticipation. I pulled on it until it stood up hard, arcing thick back toward my stomach while, a few feet from his window, my voyeur watched, still. Then, the script begun for his catharsis – my ejaculation, his vicariously – impulsively, I picked up the phone sitting on the table next to me, shuffled through some scraps of paper which it anchored until I found the number of a man I'd met the week before, and dialed.

"Still wanna taste my butt hole, Todd?" I answered low and raspy when he said "hello."

"Who is this?" he asked, his voice edged with surprise, inviting.

"We met last week." I waited. "J.O. Night. The Mineshaft."

The line was silent for a second. Then his phone clanged as though he were about to hang it up – or as though he banged it lying down, readying for a talk.

"Yeah, I'll eat your ass," he growled, "bury my tongue in that nice, warm hole."

"I bet you'd like to smell my ass-sweat, wouldn't you?" I stuck my finger up my butt, as he'd done at the bar the night we met – straining at the evening's j.o. rules, safe sex, the weekly, one-night ban on bodily fluids. "I'm fuckin' myself with my finger," I taunted. "And then I'm gonna put it right below my nose so I can sniff it while I jerk my cock." I covered my nose with my hand, breathed the aroma deeply, loudly so he could hear.

"I wanna hide my face in your ass," he sighed, "and taste that salty crack."

The man across the street had moved up to his window. His knees were bent against the sill. He gazed at me as though he knelt before an idol which he might not touch. He was beating off, feverish in a purging rite.

"The man across the way is watching me," I breathed into the phone. "Working his prick real hard. I'm gonna let him see me fuck myself. I got that butt smell right below my nose, wiped it on my moustache so I can lap it up, keep on licking it. And now I'm gonna shove my finger in and out of my hole, pretend that it's your tongue." I rammed my finger up my ass. The head of my cock swelled tight until it burned. "You're gonna fuck me with your mouth until I shoot, tongue me, jam it up me hard. Then I'm gonna turn around and piss all over you," I cried, " – wash that ass smell off your face. *You hear me!*"

"*I want you,*" Todd groaned, like a man submerged below the first wave of an opiate.

The light across the street went out.

The Pits

T. R. WITOMSKI

One of the first men I got it on with regularly was a hunky car mechanic named Jack. (My life seems to have been based on a script by Boyd McDonald.) Jack, naturally, thought that deodorant, after-shave lotion, and "all that shit" was "fag stuff." (How some guys can have frequent – not to mention incessant – sex with other men and still put down "fags" is one of the great mysteries of the cosmos, right up there with why the Post Office takes four days to deliver a letter across town.) Jack wasn't a big fan of bathing, either – in marked contrast to myself, who in the early 1970s was spending so much time at the baths that I felt like the cleanest homosexual in America.

Anyway, back in the days when it was kosher to do so, I was sucking off Jack on Mondays, Wednesdays, and alternate Fridays. I liked him because he was a pornographic cliche: "Not classically handsome, but so fuckin' masculine that I got a hard-on whenever I saw him. He had long curly black hair, a delightfully muscular body, and a huge, uncut cock that was sheer perfection." But since Jack's sexual imagination was limited (fuck this niceness – I've changed his name – his sexual imagination was retarded), there was little variety in what we actually did and called sex. I'd suck him off. Period.

Though many panegyrics have been written on cocksucking (I've done my share of them), the sad truth is that cocksucking, after the first sixty seconds or so, is boring. Boring, boring, boring. Tedious. Ennui-inducing. Dull. Boring. Even the "payoff" – "cupfuls and cupfuls of hot creamy delicious manjism" – let's all admit it – isn't what it's cracked up to be in the wild and wonderful world of smut. If those "safe sex guidelines" have shown us anything, it's certainly that "greedily gulping down a huge load of steaming cum" was never really all that thrilling to begin with.

Back to me sucking Jack's cock: my mind would wander. I'd think about what I needed from the supermarket. I'd plot revenge on editors. I'd make up new lies to tell my parents about why I wasn't married. And then one day with Jack's cock down my throat, I began to think of his armpits. I have no idea to this day why I suddenly became infatuated with armpits. There is, of course, the pornographic explanation: "Jack's densely hairy armpits exuded the most erotic macho smell. From the very first time I snuck my nose into his pits, I was totally dedicated to this very special part of a man's body." That rationale doesn't have much to do with real life (what actually happened was that Jack told me to stop screwing around and suck) but it does play in Peoria.

I'm just weird, the polite word for which is "kinky." But on quite a few occasions, as I was amusing myself with armpits, kissing and licking and slurping and having a grand old time, those guys whose pits I was so obviously entranced by didn't think me kinky. They thought me weird. And when some number is screaming, "What the fuck are you doing? Stop! It tickles/hurts/sickens me," it isn't the time to quote from Havelock Ellis's *Studies in the Psychology of Sex:* "Even in ordinary, normal persons, personal odor tends to play a not inconsiderable part in sexual attraction .... [W]hen personal odor acts as an allurement, it is the armpit ... which chiefly comes into play." Or to note that Alex Comfort in *The Joy of Sex* maintains that natural smell – a combination of the odors of the crotch, the skin, the hair, and the armpits – is "the greatest sexual asset after ... beauty." According to Comfort, "Far more human loves and antipathies are based on smell than our deodorant-and-aftershave culture admits. Many people ... say that when it's a question of bed or not bed, they let their noses lead them."

Though my work in the better sex journals on the subject of armpits has been acclaimed in certain very select circles, I've always found it a bit unseemly to pull out my clippings at a bar and force a potential trick to try in the dim light to read:

> It's a pity that we supposedly sophisticated people don't learn a few things from "primitive" cultures. For example, the Polynesians have a healthy attitude toward body odors as a sexual stimulant. According to anthropologist William Davenport, virtually all of these South Pacific islanders practice what is called the "Oceanic kiss." This, Professor Davenport reports, "consists of gently touching cheek to cheek or nose to nose and inhaling deeply so as to sense the other's odor." In those societies where this form of kiss is an essential part of lovemaking, the mouth-to-mouth kiss is seen as "disgusting." So, as the saying goes, it's all a matter of taste – or smell.
>
> Paying sexual attention to the lips, the cock, the tits, and the ass is accepted. Even an erotic interest in feet is thought "normal." But we armpit lovers are considered "far-out." Why?
>
> Anti-armpit bias seems to be simply a product of the times. If everyone was into natural-smelling armpits, the deodorant manufacturers would go bankrupt. As I delved into the literature of erotica, I discoverd the taboo against the armpit as a legitimate erogenous zone is of fairly recent origin. Historically, the axilla (the Latin word for armpit) has been an object of sexual attraction since earliest recorded time. The *Kama Sutra*, the famous Indian sex manual, refers to the armpit as a suitable place for kissing, stroking, licking and other forms of stimulation. Chinese and Arabic sex guides concur.
>
> Furthermore, archeologists have unearthed statues from ancient Greece and Rome that show muscular men with arms raised and underarms exposed in a sexually exciting manner. And the great painters have also shown an awareness of the sensuality of the male armpit. In past centuries, a man's armpits probably ranked right along with his cock and ass in terms of erotic appeal.
>
> Summer is the prime season for armpit watchers like myself. Guys in tank tops are an inexhaustible source of erotic fascination, but I'm especially turned-on by men who wear regular t-shirts that are cut so close on the arms that a few puffs of armpit hair poke out provocatively. And sweat stains under the arms! Is there anything sexier than a hot stud with two large blotches of armpit fluid adorning his shirt? I'm hard just thinking about it...

Don't go away. The hot part is coming up.

Last summer economic necessity forced me to teach a course

at a local community college in creative writing, a subject I knew absolutely nothing about, which is why I was qualified to teach it. Before the first class, I swore to my politically correct friends on a stack of *Christopher Streets* that I would not even think about having sex with one (or horror of horrors, more than one) of my students. But God decided to test my resolve by putting Michael in my class. God won.

I know that today's in-the-know gays hold it as a sacred truth (first revealed to Randy Shilts in Dave's Baths) that responsible sex proceeds from a loving relationship between two wonderful people. But since I am by no means a wonderful person, it should not be surprising that I didn't want to have a relationship, loving or otherwise, with Michael. I wanted to use him as an object to satisfy my weird lust. I wanted his armpits.

Of course, it was all Michael's fault. I didn't *make* him jog to class in an old t-shirt and cut-offs, working up a healthy sweat on the way. Since I could see his sublime pits through his sweat-soaked shirt, whatever enthusiasm I might have mustered for my students' work rapidly waned. I longed to tell all of them that not only were they hopeless as writers, but that they were distracting me from devoting my full attention to contemplation of Michael's armpits. The world could survive without the short stories of Cynthia Gregory and the poems of Adolf Borris, but I could not survive without carnal knowledge of Michael's pits.

Did I really use such a tired line as "Michael, can I see you after class a moment"? I fear I did. And did Michael betray his innocence (which only made his armpits even more attractive to me) by replying "Sure thing"? I fear he did.

So we chatted. Which wasn't all that easy since I had not actually gotten around to reading anything he'd written. (I had, however, smelled the papers he'd turned in – sadistic bitch that I am, I required 2000 words a week minimum from each of my students, a task which would be beyond my own capabilities – and they were definitely all A+.) And since I had already shown I had no way with words, I had nothing to lose (I had, after all, already committed Carterian lust with Michael) by coming out with *this* classic, drop-dead pick-up line: "How 'bout a beer at my place?"

The terrible state of American higher education is due in no small part to the fact that people like me are allowed to teach. Why hadn't it dawned on me that a school that would have me for a teacher was a school I shouldn't have wanted to teach in? And what, if anything, could Michael possibly learn in such a college? He certainly hadn't learned *not* to accompany sleazy teachers to their apartments.

In the war zone that passes for my apartment, my end of the conversation was rather stilted: Michael wanted to talk about writing, specifically *my* writing ("What's it feel like to be so widely published?" "Like a lifetime devoted to eating ice with impacted wisdom teeth.), but I couldn't get my mind off his pits. Michael was dark-skinned and densely hairy; the parts of his body not covered by his skimpy attire were a virtual forest of hair. I had found nirvana, and he wanted to talk shop.

Though I have tried mightily, I have never found a good way to say, "Could we stop talking now and have sex, and, by the way, are you gay?" Let alone a good way to say "Let's leave writing and move on to armpits." Luckily, my planets were correctly positioned (or something) because Michael said, "Do you think I should write about my gay experiences?"

Bingo!

To my credit, I did not say, "I don't give a fuck what you write about, but I'd be most receptive to you experiencing some gay sex. As in right here, right now."

Now that sex had reared its head, I was on surer conversational ground. I also had enough beer in the refrigerator to guarantee that sex talk would eventually lead to armpit action. Budweiser and armpits — what a combination! Do the Anheuser-Busch people know this?

After the fourth beer, Michael and I were snuggling close together. After the fifth beer, we were heavily engaged in deep, passionate kissing and lusty body groping. I slipped my hands underneath his shirt and up to his hairy, damp armpits. Just feeling those long, silky strands of pit hair made my pulse rate increase (I'll give myself a heart attack doing this stuff one of these days) and the bulge in my pants grew larger by the second.

Michael and I struggled to our feet, still clawing at each other (Michael eager to get points on the student scale for making it with a teacher, me eager to have a *serious* go at his pits). We tried to stagger to the bedroom. We never made it there. (I almost never have sex in the bedroom, but my couch is severely cum-stained. It would be logical to move the bed into the living room and the couch into the bedroom, but — let's face it — a guy who's into armpits ain't logical.)

Hot parts start now:

I dropped to my knees and pulled Michael's shorts down, revealing a funky jockstrap that couldn't quite conceal all of his thick crop of pubic hair. Overcome with desire, I pulled the jock down and pressed my face deep into his aromatic crotch.

As I looked up, I saw a sight that nearly made me shoot off right then and there. Michael was pulling his t-shirt over his head, and as he did so the copious hair under his arms was finally fully revealed in all its glory.

For a moment I thought of disengaging myself from his crotch in order to devote my oral attentions to the two magnificent pools of fur under his arms (*pools of fur!* — now we know: old porno writers don't die, they come up with "pools of fur"). But I decided that it would heighten the experience (and lengthen this story) if I worked my way up to my ultimate goal.

Quickly stripping off our clothes, I pushed Michael back to the couch, spread his muscular legs, and dove on his huge, hairy balls, sucking them until his moans reached a crescendo. Never losing sight of my ultimate destination, my mouth left his nuts, heavy with his jism, and I licked a slippery trail up the length of his body, pausing for a good long while to suck on his small, hard nipples.

I kissed his mouth passionately, so that the taste from his crotch was now on both our lips. Then I pushed his arms up so that they were fully extended and buried my nose and mouth in those incredible patches of hair. Michael's armpit odor was intoxicating. Inhaling his body's perfume effected me the way sniffing cocaine would effect other people. His delectable smell lingered in my nostrils as I stroked, kissed, and nibbled in his pits, twining the juicy strands of hair around my fingers.

In a hoarse whisper, Michael breathed into my ear, "I think I've got an idea you'd like." Had I found a fellow armpit aficionado? Or merely someone who scrupulously read the better sex journals?

Deftly massaging the shaft of my cock with his hand, Michael laid back on the couch and pulled me up so that my cockhead was against his moist pit. The sensation of his wiry hair sweeping across my cock was fantastic – it felt like he was tickling my dick with a fine paintbrush. I pushed my cock against his pit. I was just starting to get into a good rhythm, with Michael's hand applying just the right amount of pressure on my shaft, when he abruptly changed position. Raising himself on his right elbow, Michael moved my cock under his left armpit, which he then lowered so that my cock was encased in a tunnel formed by his arm and the side of his chest.

As I started to fuck Michael's armpit, I reached down to his crotch and gently stroked his stiff prick. I was so fuckin' turned-on that I could do nothing by stroke faster. I knew that I couldn't hold back much longer, and from Michael's panting moans, I could tell that he was close to climax too. As I shouted the *pro forma* announcement that I was coming, Michael squeezed his arm on my back stroke, then opened slightly to allow me one last push before I released a geyser of cum.

At precisely the moment of my ejaculation, Michael raised his arm so that I could see my jism splatter over his hairy pit. I thought I'd never stop coming. When my orgasmic moans subsided, I rubbed my cock in Michael's cum-soaked underarm, my hand pulling his cock until his load flew out of his piss-slit.

Does everybody understand now why I've become such a dedicated teacher of creative writing at the local community college?

Phone Today!

ERIC ROFES

I'd seen the advertisement before in my favorite smut magazines – *Honcho, Stallion, Mandate, Drummer* – but I'd always breezed over it and all the other ads for phone jerk-off services. I got off looking at the burly construction workers and hunky body builders, but I couldn't imagine myself picking up the telephone and making the call. I don't know if it was because I tend to be a little phone shy or because I'm cautious with my credit cards, but the thought of talking to some presumably hot stranger and beating my meat while connected by Ma Bell, just didn't appeal to my erotic impulses.

Something changed that night. I don't know whether it was my mood or my circumstances, but when I flipped through the pink pages of the current *Advocate*, the large display advertisement jumped out at me. "Get Hot With Some Hot Men!", proclaimed the ad, illustrated with a photo of a naked man's butt and legs entangled in his telephone cord. "Phone Today!" it urged, listing a number in San Francisco for Sex Link, a 24-hour a day service. Two sample illustrations of MasterCard and Visa plates in the advertisement's lower-right corner made it apparent that I could gain immediate access to this phone service.

Christ, Rick, I thought to myself, don't let yourself get caught up in one of these sleazy, irreputable sex businesses. I recalled the time I sent away for some dirty magazines while I was still a teenager living at home and for years after I moved out my name must have darted onto one mailing list after another, because everytime I'd come home for a visit a large quantity of "plain brown wrappers" were awaiting me. I thought about the time I'd summoned up the courage to run a simple personal advertisement in our local weekly newspaper, using my college dormitory as the return address, and had to explain to my roommates why our postbox was deluged for weeks with mail addressed simply to "Ricky." And then there were all those times I'd given my correct number to strangers I'd meet in bars only to be unable to place the name with the face the following week and got myself into some pretty uncomfortable situations with some pretty unappealing guys. No, let's keep this simple, I told myself. Phone sex services seem like a bizarre erotic outlet that would be more trouble than they're worth.

I flipped the pages back to the personals pages and jerked myself off reading about a "Hot College Jock" who was seeking "heavy action with young kid brother," and fantasizing about myself messing around with this guy. I tossed the newspaper onto the table, and tossed aside all thoughts of phone sex with sweaty men in hard-hats. Or so I thought.

For the next day or so, at odd times, I'd find myself getting horny and getting frustrated with the limited options available to me. Ordinarily that would sound like a strange remark coming from me. I'm considerd quite a hot-looking guy, with the dark, Italian looks that seem to drive a lot of gay guys wild. When I'm feeling sorry for myself, I gripe about the promincence of my nose, the shortness of my stature (5'9") or the fact that I'm so hairy that I have regularly found myself prey to men with bizarre hair fetishes. But I'm not dumb and I know that the fact that I've worked myself into a tight, muscular body, and my sexy ethnic looks keep all kinds of men on my tail. Since I make my home in the gay ghetto of Pittsburgh – and since I spend my share of time at a primarily gay Nautilus center – I've got more than my share of opportunities to tumble with some pretty good-looking guys. So why was I feeling frustrated?

The answer is simple. His name is Jonathan Shapiro. He's the man I'd always dreamed of meeting and I met him six months ago at the Nautilus center. Tall, dark and handsome, with a big Jewish nose to match my own, he swept me off my feet and out of my shorts after following me home from the gym one September night. Our courtship was romantic and intense: a dozen long-stemmed roses on my birthday, long, soul-searching conversations while walking by the river, and a mad animal drive toward one another that led us to weekends in bed with the phone off the hook. On New Year's Day we moved in together and, since that time, we've successfully attempted to keep ourselves monogamous.

Monogamy might translate as "monotony" to many people but we haven't found it that way. We're not so naive as to think that we're going to spend the rest of our lives balling only with one another. We've agreed that, for the next year, neither of us would sleep with anyone else. This would allow us to direct our sexual energies to one another, deepen the sexual bond between us, and give us more time together. After a year, we're planning on assessing the success of monogamy and deciding whether we want to continue.

Another consideration in our minds when we decided to be monogamous was AIDS. While I don't think either Jonathan or I could be considered obsessed with health matters, we both work on our local AIDS committee and have developed a decent consciousness concerning sensible sex. Our sex life has developed wonderfully with a vigilant eye toward reducing our risk for disease. When we're together, there's a sense of concern and trust that unfortunately isn't always there when you pick up a trick on the street. So for this year at least, we're pledged to monogamy.

So, why was I feeling sexually frustrated. Why was that phone sex advertisement darting in and out of my mind? Why did I pick up the pink pages again two night later and begin to read the fine print?

Jonathan Shapiro is an airline pilot and his schedule takes him away for four days at a time and then sends him home for four days. That evening, as I glanced over the advertisement for Sex Link, my lover was somewhere over the Pacific Ocean, heading for

Tokyo. As I read the information in the advertisement and felt the excitement pulse into my cock, Jonathan Shapiro was reading aviation charts and monitoring the pulse of the radar mappings.

"Hook yourself up with other hot, horny guys through our 24-hour phone service," read the fine print. "Our computer will connect you with men calling from all over the country, looking to meet you, feel each other out over the phone, or get off with one another, even though you may be thousands of miles apart. No trained actors will answer your call: You'll speak with diverse guys with diverse tastes from diverse places for less than $3 an hour." The price surprised me. I assumed phone sex services cost thirty or forty bucks a call. Maybe I should give it a call?

I wondered what kind of person would answer the phone at the number in the ad. I imagined some kind of hostile, judgmental guy, taking your name, credit card number and phone number while chuckling to himself, "Here's another loser, jerking off on the phone because he can't make it in bars." Since I was normally a bit shy over the phone, I wondered if I could deal with the hostile tone of voice and the leering questions. Would he ask me what I was into? Would I have to describe myself physically to him over the phone? And did I want "Sex Link Phone Sex Service, Inc." to appear on my credit card statement each month?

I went and ahead and called, despite my fears. The phone rang once and then was answered by a deep, friendly voice accented with a bit of Southern twang. "Hello, welcome to Sex Link Phone Service. This is Jim speaking, may I help you?"

"Um, yes," I mumbled awkwardly. "I'm calling to find out about how your phone service works."

"Sure. Where did you find our number?"

"I read an advertisement in the *Advocate* pink pages."

"Great. If you'll hold on for a moment, I'm going to play a recording that gives you the basic information on how we do things here at Sex Link. If you listen to the recording and are interested in signing on as a member, give us a call at the office number, 415-302-4353. Now hold on while I switch on the recording."

The line seemed to go dead for a moment, but I held on as Jim had instructed. Suddenly some tinny music came over the line and an obviously upbeat recorded voice began its rap.

"Welcome to Sex Link, a twenty-four-hour-a-day telephone service for cruising other guys, making dates, creating your own erotic phone fantasies, or simply talking to another hot guy. If you are eighteen years old or over, we hope you'll consider joining 2,000 other men from every state and several foreign countries who enjoy our computer-connected services.

"The way it works is as follows. You call our phone line and our computer immediately links you with the next available caller on the line. From there on out it's up to you — once you've been connected, go for it! Our only rule is that if you wish to disconnect from whomever you're speaking with, politely say goodbye before hanging up.

"For a few cents a day, you may make use of our three phone lines, provided you have access to a touch-tone telephone. Sex Link is easy-to-use, safe, and fully confidential. You may join by using your MasterCard or Visa, or by sending a check or money order. Our office number is 415-302-4353. If you can handle the fantasy, check it out now."

The voice dissolved into the music. I seized a pen from the nightstand next to the bed and jotted the number onto a corner of the pink page ad. Then I hung up the telephone.

I thought for a moment. I'm over eighteen. I have a touch-tone phone. I'm pretty polite over the phone. This would be a good outlet for me to use when Jonathan's flying.

I decided to give it a go. I pushed the buttons for the Sex Link office and again reached a friendly voice. "Sex Link office, Mark speaking," he said in a voice that made me wonder if Mark were a college student working his way through school by staffing the phone sex office. "Are you interested in becoming a member?"

"Yes, I am."

"Where are you calling from?"

"I'm calling from Pittsburgh, Pennsylvania."

"Have you ever used Sex Link before?"

"No, I haven't."

"Do you have a touch-tone telephone?"

"Yes, I do."

"Please push number one on your telephone."

I leaned over and pressed the number one. The tone rang on the line. I supposed he was checking it out to make certain I wasn't lying about the touch-tone.

"As a member of Sex Link, you can get ten hours of talk time for $25 or twenty hours for $50. When you get down to an hour or less remaining, we will give you a call and let you know you'll need to resubscribe. If it is not okay to call you at home, we wait until you call in and then we break into the computer before your line is linked to someone else. Would you prefer the ten or twenty hour option?"

I thought for a moment. Ten seemed safer and, besides, I was only planning on using this on those rare occasions when a dirty magazine didn't fill my need. "I'll take ten hours, please."

"Will you be paying by credit card, check or money order?"

I supposed it would be easiest to put this on my Master Card, but I didn't want my statement to expose my lewd pastimes. "If I put this on my credit card, what will the notation read?"

"It'll read simply 'Link Services, Inc.'. Or would you rather we notate yours with 'Hot Sex Phone Line'?!" he joked.

"Well, as long as that's all it says, I'll put it on my MasterCard."

"We'll need your name, address, phone number, card number and expiration date, please."

I slowly gave him the information he'd requested. "You're not going to send me any mail are you?" I asked, wondering how I'd be explaining this venture to my lover.

"Not if you'd prefer us not to. Would you prefer us not to call you as well to remind you when you're running low on time?"

"Yes, I'd rather you just break into the line when I call the computer."

"That's fine with us. Many of our members prefer that kind of confidentiality. Now grab a pen because I'm going to give you the two numbers to use to get onto our system, along with your personal code. We have two lines, one is a specialized line for S&M and the other is a general phone line. You may use one or the other or both." He then proceeded to give me the numbers, along with my own identification number.

"When you call one of our two lines, you'll have to wait for a moment. Then you'll hear a tone. When you hear the tone, simply punch in your code number as if you were making a regular call. Once your code number is entered, you'll either hear two short rings and someone will be on the line or you'll hear nothing until someone else calls in on the line and then you'll hear the two short rings and someone will join you on the line. You two take it from there."

While he presented all this information in a clear way with a calm voice, I was getting confused. I asked him to repeat the information and he did.

"Remember," he cautioned. "You are subject to removal from our membership for rudeness. It's the only rule we have. It only takes a few seconds to politely say goodbye if you don't want to continue talking." He paused here for a moment. "I think that's all the information you need. Any questions?"

I couldn't think of any. "You mean, all I have to do is dial one of these numbers, wait for the tone, punch in my code number and wait for the rings?"

"That's correct, just wait for those two fabulous rings."

"And it costs me only $25 for ten hours – plus, of course, the phone charges between here and San Francisco?"

"That's right, and you can talk to your phone company about some of their cost-saving coast-to-coast rates."

"Well then, I think I'm all set to go. Thanks a lot for your help, Mark."

"Thank you, Rick. You're all set. Have a nice day and enjoy Sex Link!"

I didn't make my first call that night. I think I felt so titillated – and so naughty – that I went to bed, feeling like a little kid who just stole Mama's pies from the oven. Before I fell asleep I imagined myself making these phone calls, giggling at my attempt to make my voice even deeper. Jonathan would get a real kick out of my new tactic for staying faithful.

It was on the following night – with Jonathan due to fly in just twenty-four hours later – that the urge seized me. I shuffled through the magazines on the nightstand to find the phone numbers and codes that I'd been given the night before. After locating the slip of paper, I turned down the lights, turned on the stereo, and settled back on the bed.

I pulled the phone onto my lap and dialed the number for the phone sex line. Immediately, I heard the tone that I'd been told to expect. Referring back to the sheet, I punched in my code number. There was a moment's pause – I wondered if I'd not completed entering the code – and then two short rings.

"Hello?" a gruff-sounding but friendly voice at the other end said to me.

"Hello," I answered matter-of-factly.

"What's your name, buddy?" he asked.

"Rick," I responded. "What's your?"

"Tony. Where're you calling from?"

"Pittsburgh, Pennsylvania."

"I'm calling from Houston. What're you lookin' for, Rick?" he asked.

This caught me by surprise. What *was* I looking for?

"I guess I'm looking to get off," I answered quietly.

"Good," he said. "I'm lookin' to get off too. I've got my big, fat dick out and I'm pumpin' it with my hand. You got your cock out?"

"Um, no, I don't," I answered, taking my hand immediately to my fly and quickly unbuttoning my 501s.

"Well take it out buddy," he said roughly. "I want to hear you beating that meat of yours."

His voice was turning me on. By the time I got my cock out of my pants, my eight inch shaft was throbbing between my fingers.

"It's out now," I said.

"Good. What do you look like, Rick?"

What the shit does it matter what I look like? This is probably part of the fantasy trip for some guys.

"I'm 5'9" tall, weigh 165 pounds, I have black hair, brown eyes, a lot of body hair. I've got a 40 inch chest and a 32 inch waist."

"Are you clean-shaven?" he asked.

"Yeah. I used to have a moustache but I shaved it a few months ago."

"You sound hot."

"What do you look like?" I asked.

"I'm tall, dark, and kinda mean looking. I'm 6'2", 190 pounds. I have brown curly hair, brown eyes, a short beard. I'm well-built, 44 inch chest, 34 inch waist. I've got a big, thick cock with big low hanging balls. Any questions?"

"How old are you?" I asked.

"Thirty-five. And you?"

"Twenty-nine."

"You sound real hot," he said. I could hear his breathing deepen as he stroked his cock.

"So do you," I answered. My cock was fully-hard now and the head was starting to ooze pre-cum.

"What are you doing with your cock?"

"I'm jerking on it," I answered. "I'm playing with my big dick and gettin' off on it."

"I'm strokin' my big meat too. Feels good . . . feels *real* good."

He paused here for a moment. I wasn't sure what to say. For a few seconds we just breathed heavy at one another. Then he started talking again.

"Are you drippin' yet?" he asked.

"Yeah. My cock's drippin' thin strands of cum. My hand's getting nice and wet and sticky."

"What do you want me to do for that cock?" he asked.

"Oh, man," I was getting close. "I'd like you to reach down and take my cock in your meaty hands and start pumping me. I'd like you to pump my cock with your fist."

"Yeah," he said between breaths. "Yeah, buddy. I'm grabbin' at your crotch. Feel my fingers rakin' through the hair. Feel my fingers circle around your hard, stiff, thick cock. Yeah. Feel my fingers press against the shaft. I'm moving up and down your cock now, strokin' you nice, man. I'm strokin' your dick nice. Feel me jerkin' at your dick. How's that feel buddy? How's your big dick feel between my fingers?"

I could swear I could feel his hand grabbing at my prick. "It feels good, man. It feels real good having you jerkin' me off."

"Yeah, it feels good to me too. It feels good squeezin' your cock, squeezin' it tight. It feels good pumpin' your meat with one hand while I'm pumpin' mine with the other hand."

"Oh man," I gasped, "I'm gettin' pretty close."

"Hold on for a second," he ordered. "I want us to shoot our loads together."

"Okay, man," I felt the sweat break out on my forehead and I let go of my cock for a moment.

"I'm gonna go up and chew on your tit a little bit with my mouth," he threatened. "I'm gonna bite that hard little tit of yours."

"Oh god, man. Oh Christ. Shit, man. I can feel you bitin' me."

"Yeah. Yeah. I'm bitin' your tit. Feel my teeth nip at it. Nippin' at that hard pec of yours. Lickin' that tit. Chewin' on it. Bitin' it. Rubbin' my beard against your tit and that fuckin' hairy chest."

"Oh shit, man. I'm gonna cum – "

"Me too, man. I'm gonna shoot. Let me just bite that tit hard now. Let me just take it between my lips and suck the livin' shit out of your tit, boy. Yeah. Oh, yeah. Here I come, boy. Get ready for me to shoot my load all over that fuckin' hairy chest of yours."

I felt the heat rise through my own loins and begin to erupt in spasms. The cum shot suddenly from my hard, thick cock, flooding in streaks across my belly and my chest.

"Oh shit!" I heard him yell. "Oh, fuck. I'm shootin'. I'm shootin'. Oh shit, boy, take my fuckin' load. Take my fuckin' load all over your fuckin' tits. Oh, shit. Fuck, shit. Take it, boy. Take it."

My cock kept shooting in small spasms over my torso. The thick, pearly seed mixing in with the dense hair that covers me.

I didn't hear anything at the other end of the phone line. Finally, I heard his labored breathing.

"Are you there, Rick?" he asked.

"Yeah, Tony. You okay?"

"Sure, man. You're one fuckin' hot guy."

"You are too."

"Well, I hope I'll catch you again on the phone line. Remember, Tony from Houston."

"Yeah, thanks."

"Catch you later buddy."

I heard the phone disconnect and I was left cradling a receiver playing the dial tone in my ear. Goodnight, Tony from Houston. Goodnight, Jonathan in Tokyo.

A satisfied smile crept over my face as I felt the cum drying on my chest. Thanks to Ma Bell, I had a new way to release my horniness and keep myself out of trouble. I wonder if any of those male operators were listening in?

Love at First Flight

DAVID BARTON—JAY

They were only a minute or two away from take-off, and the seat next to Dale was still empty. Great, he thought, more room to spread the knees apart on the long, cramped flight to London. A quick glance around revealed that that was the only seat so destined to be vacant. Smiling inside at the goodness of his luck, he buckled his safety belt up as required and shut his tired eyes down to rest.

A momentary delay was announced: A last-minute laggard, with a boarding pass problem, was on his way up from the terminal. He brought his outstretched knees in a bit, grimacing that deep within he had secretly suspected it was too, too good to be true. But as the latecomer, big and breathless, bolted down the aisle, he soon realized that Ms. Lady Luck had favored him after all. To say that the last man in was to be the handsomest of them all, would be to understate. For the next few seconds, Dale entered a lovely trance.

At the hurried direction of an annoyed flight attendant, he lumbered toward his seat, obviously embarrassed by all of the unwanted attention that had been focused upon him. Dale had decided that he was fairly close to his own age – somewhere between a virile thirty-five and a finally-getting-it-together-forty. As he reached up to open the overhead compartment, looking happy to be ridding himself of his bulky carry-on baggage, his tightly stretched deep green sweater separated just far enough away from the waist of his jeans to give Dale a beautiful blink at the tempting, masculine down that had grown near his navel. The elastic band of his underpants was not visible, and considering the possibility that he wasn't wearing any was somewhat of an erotic amusement.

Taken so absolutely by the look of him, he didn't think quickly enough to stand to allow the new man easy access to his seat. The courtesy not having been offered, he dove directly ahead to accomplish the awkward act of squeezing by. Barely audible, and a bit bashful, he strung *pardon*, *excuse* and *forgive me*, all together, and practically pushed his banquet-quality butt smack into Dale's face while doing so. Dale, having been a hole hog from way back, became intoxicated at just the mere thought of what a friendly little sniff in there might be like: d'dark, d'damp, d'licious, to be sure! And don't doubt at all that if he could have, he would have frozen the pouncing passerby right there while his nose was still aimed at his anus, more ready than ever to become lost in the ecstasy of lapping it right up until the very moment they were scheduled to land at Heathrow. Great theme for a dirty movie, Dale thought, as he took a deep but dismal breath back to reality.

Moments like this had become rare for Dale, in that for more than two years now, due to the fear of The Deadly Disease, all of his sexual activity had come to a screeching halt. It had nothing to do at all with his willpower; simply, he was scared to death. But oh, how he used to suck on ass. It was forever the main dish during all of his countless sexual feasts, and he realized right then that his appetite for it had not yet been lost. Thoughts of those bittersweet and succulent little openings still inspired him like nothing else ever could. He could take dicks or leave dicks, but it was always the tight and tiny heiny hole that was home. He valued the control he had been able to exercise in refraining, but nontheless, the next half hour was spent in trying to remember what the last asshole he had eaten had tasted like.

It had been Matthew's, and it had been their last time together. The sex was never all that great (Matt was too passive, unable to perform the aggressive turnabout which Dale required), but his ass and the hole that was in it was the best ever. It wasn't just the porno-mag perfection of it, or even the little-boy-like hairlessness of it. It was the inebriating smell of it. Whatever the chemical composition of the oils of Matt's body was, when combined with the stale, salty sweat that gathered inside that wonderful little circle of delicate creases, it made Dale spin. Those were the days, he thought, those were the days. The days of lovers and of loving; the days of having and of holding. Delirious days of aromatic armpits and arousing assholes. Those were the days of hot pricks pissing and hard pricks pounding. Yep, he recalled, those were the days.

In the meantime, the plane had taken off without his thinking about it, so contained was he within his own thoughts. Orders for drinks were being taken, magazines and those doll-house-size pillows were being distributed. Up to that time, all that had gone between the two travelers was a little nod coupled with a cursory smile, but soon that was to change. Dale had reached down for the book he had brought to read, one of Italo Calvino's magical ones, and the man now seated next to him plunged right in. He told Dale that he had just finished reading one of his books, the first he'd experienced, and expressed the joys he had in it. It wasn't just a line; he was very specific about some of his favorite details, many of the same ones that Dale remembered enjoying also. And before long, the book was closed. Their names were exchanged, at which point they broke into guarded but genuine laughter. The most silly and absurd coincidence had taken place: Dale found himself sitting next to a man named Hill, short for Hillard. Hillard Thomas Woodhall. There they were, Hill and Dale. Hill was reminded – and reported immediately – of a neighbor of his with the surname of Field, who had taken a business partner named Streem. Although it wasn't spelled as is the artery of water, it had always been good for a chuckle. And it was again at that moment.

His accent was beautifully British. He was returning home from a visit with his younger brother, an officer at the British Consulate in D.C., and his new wife, a librarian in a nearby univeristy in Virginia. Dale explained that he was taking a vacation, but he quickly reworded himself in keeping with his destination and his temporary companion, saying rather that he was *on holiday*. It prompted another giggle and continued to prove they were happy to have found each other.

It was a good while after that initial conversation, small talk really, until they spoke again. It was when dinner was delivered, such as it was. Again there was reason for laughter: one dull dinner roll, little meat chunks of a curious color soaking in a dreary-looking gravy, a small, pale, gathering of peas, a hapless boiled potato of miniscule size garnished with a lifeless fragment of parsley, a puddle of something neither of them could identify, and a little square of white cake covered with an orange-colored icing that made the dessert course completely resistable. They chatted as they picked, they drank as they chatted, and their knees came to rest heavily on each other's. There was no attempt by either of them to alter the physical circumstance. It became obvious that they were both being quite deliberate about it. They smiled knowingly, shook hands discreetly once again, this time taking a good long time to withdraw. Dale's penis had stirred, and Hill's piece was already stone-shamelessly-hard. Their eyes engaged for a while in "that look," and it was almost romantic.

Well, what is it that one does with a handsome, well-hardened Englishman on a crowded flight across the Atlantic? You guessed it, almost nothing – except, of course, to talk carefully and touch inconspicuously, always mindful of being in view of those around them. After exchanging some additional personal details, Hill suggested, rather than chance being overheard, that they correspond via notes. Another giggle was heard as both of them reached for some paper. For Hill, it was a yellow legal pad; for Dale, a small wire-bound notebook. Dale offered to start first, as each of them arranged their little "convenience trays" just over their laps. Then, not unlike two children at school, they prepared to compose. It had been years since either of them had passed notes to "boyhood sweethearts," and being about to do so brought back some very pleasant memories.

Every once in a while, Hill tried to sneak a peek over Dale's shoulder, but it was soon understood that such behaviour would be disallowed. Dale's letter read like this:

Dear Hillard, I can't believe I am about to sit here and write an obscene note to a total stranger sitting next to me. My current preoccupation with the AIDS crisis has me stopped on all fronts (all fronts, get it?), but when your well-made ass passed by my face as you climbed over me on your way to your seat, all hell broke loose in my head. I wanted to stick my horny tongue right up into it and suck you out there until we landed. Right now I'm sitting here, hard as rock, thinking of how it would taste. Of perfume? Of powder? Or of more natural causes? Would it be bitter? Would it be sweet? Would there be any anal hair there? As you can tell, you have really boiled up my juices.

It was signed: Love at first flight, Dale.

He folded it, blushed slightly, smiled, and handed it to Hill whose left hand had, by then, found its way into Dale's lap. It was grope time; it had been ages! What Hill found, as he started to read the note now unfolded in front of him, was quite something. Although he never liked considering himself a "size queen," and, in fact, actually hated the term, when presented with a cock like this one was, he knew he fit the description perfectly. His hand was wrapped around a cock that was not only of lavish length, but was of great girth as well. In plain English, he had landed himself one big dick! He held on to it tightly, as though to Dear Life itself. Dale, ready to explode, moved it gently away. Now Dale's right leg, and Hill's left, had crossed at their calves. Hill prepared his response:

Dear Dale, I should like very much to give you a crack at my asshole (crack, get it?). There isn't any perfume to be found there, nor is there any powder. My guess is that it's still smelling sweet, but getting more and more seasoned with every second. Insofar as the hairs there are concerned, they are shaved away at all times, a ritual I've been practicing for years. It would be an honor to have you there, but what can we safely do?

There was a brief postscript: Oh, how I'd love to picnic for a while about that monster pole of yours. Ah, well.

Dale's eyes examined the note in record time and responded:

In that the idea of eating your farting asshole must live, unfortunately, in fantasy only, and fucking with a condom fails to excite me, how about if I nose myself right in there, take my breath from it for a while, and then fill you with my fingers?

No little Groucho Marxian duck appeared from above, but to Hill, duck or no duck, "fill" had long ago become his magic word. Even before his puberty, he had become what some would term "an enema freak." From a very early age, he faked one painful stomach disorder after the other just so his "mum" would attend to his "bum." He made a hobby of fabricating all sorts of reasons just to get her to fetch the beloved red bag and bring it to him. But as an adult, he found it always difficult to work the subject of his "fetish" into a conversation. Often, opportunities were passed for fear that someone would get the wrong idea and assume incorrectly that he was into . . . uh, well, you know.

On rare occasion it would happen that he would connect somehow with another fellow who, too, as a "wee lad" had found it to be his favorite toy. Those precious enema scenes were to him what "gushers" are to Texans. For the most part it had become a sex secret he kept to himself, and a sex act he usually performed on himself. But now, with this moment at hand, he took the plunge. He wrote:

Dear Dale, Fill me? Fill me? You say you want to fill me?

Dale nodded in the affirmative and then asked, without bothering to write it out, if Hill meant what he thought he meant. There was an embarrassing pause on Hill's part, at which point Dale motioned him to write it down. By that time, however, it wasn't really necessary. This well-traveled Dale was well aware that the English were notorious enema fans.

Hill wrote only the word enema and passed it on. Dale, without unfolding the paper, wrote the word out as well. Hill sat straight up as a result, and dashed madly back to his note pad.

He laid bare:

I don't think I can last until we land; I am sure I will have to go and pop off in the john. Drawing a mental picture of you holding that big, bulging bag over me, your blood-flooded stem, rigid with pleasure, hovering, is almost too much! Yes Dale, please. Please come home with me and let me exhibit my ass. Let me stretch my legs apart quite beyond design, and let me open my hole to your whims. I have a hundred things you could push into it, but most of all, I have a very special and splendid big nozzle. It's quite old, very long, quite thick. It is black and slightly curved, and was designed originally to douche a lady. Perhaps I could lick it like I should like to lick your own long, thick nozzle. Perhaps you would place it in my mouth the way you would place your penis there. I could show you just how good a suck-mouth I can be. Perhaps I could place myself between your legs and lick away at the bursting balls hanging there. Would you like that? Would that get you going? Would you like to watch my big bare buns moving all about the bed as I strain to take every drop of the liquid being hosed into me? And then I could turn over, after having met the demand, and watch us pop well off together, your cum merging with mine, dripping all over and down my belly? Oh god, if only then you would fall on top of me so that I could hold you tight and grab onto the cheeks of your ass and press you to me! And then we could kiss by holding our faces close to one another, saving our lips for another time? Say yes. Say yes! Please say yes.

Dale waited until Hill had stripped all the covers from his private thoughts, and, forever a lover the The Happy End, he assured:

If you think you're flying now, my fiendish friend, you just wait until we land!

Champagne

JOHN PRESTON

"That's easy for you to say. You're an old man. You had all those chances . . ."

"I'm not old." That one hurt.

"Well, you're fifteen years older than I am and you did have all those chances I didn't. You went to the Mineshaft, *all the time*! You went to the bath houses *whenever you wanted to*! I bet you even . . ." his eyes half closed with a mixture of lust, envy and anger, "I bet you even *ate ass*."

"I don't know if you should be jealous just 'cause I had a whole lot of invitations to contract hepatitis – and took them and got it, twice."

"Hepatitis! Who gives a shit about hepatitis?!"

"You should. Everyone should. It was – it is – a lousy dangerous disease and we all were stupid enough to treat it like a common cold. So you did some things and you got some things, that was the attitude. But . . ."

"What was it like?" His eyes had opened up, there was an edge of wonder in his expression now.

"It was . . . hectic. Bars till four in the morning, baths, drugs, nameless bodies . . ."

"God! What I wouldn't give . . . Nameless bodies? I not only insist on a complete medical history, I have to have a number to contact in case of emergency ten years from now. Anonymous sex? I demand two pieces of identification, at least one with a picture."

He slumped back in his chair and rested his head against the wood panelled wall. He sighed, an honest sigh that relaxed his face. He was gazing out into space, there wasn't even the strain of concentration, just repose.

It was a gorgeous profile. There were times like this when I could only imagine him as a *Life* photograph, in black and white, the kind they published in the Forties. He should model, I realized, the look was coming back.

He had black hair, carefully swept back in an arc over his head but not so full nor so completely trained that it had the impression of being too well designed. It was simple hair, masculine hair.

He was clean shaven, pale in this winter weather, his skin was in stark contrast to the two ebony arcs of his eyebrows. His lips, though, were full and red. Maybe, perhaps, his head was too adult, possibly too large for the rest of his body. He was wearing his perfect clone costume – as always. Hooded sweatshirt over mandatory white t-shirt, jeans, running shoes.

"Is that why you moved away?" He asked that one suddenly, not changing his expression nor moving to look toward me.

"No, that was . . . coincidence." I was living in the country now. "It doesn't mean anything. I had a lover. We were done with the city. There were ways to make money in the country that satisfied us. So, we left."

"Where is he?" Still no eye contact. I wanted it now.

"He left. A long time ago. Years."

"Is he dead?" Now he looked at me.

"Yes, no." We were living in the middle of The Plague. When else would one man make the assumption that another's former lover was dead? And when else could a two word response convey so much: Yes, he is dead; No, he didn't die of The Disease.

"I'm sorry." We knew one another well enough already that I could tell he was sincere. He reached across the coffee shop table and took my hand; we touched each other.

"It was a long time ago. It's still there. But it was a long time ago. It happens anyway, you know." Even without The Epidemic. "People die. Others have to live."

"Let's go do some living." His face lit up a bit. He gave my hand a last squeeze and we stood up and put on our jackets.

We walked out onto the snowy sidewalk and began to move toward his apartment a few blocks away. We were in the middle of the ghetto. He didn't hesitate to wrap an arm around my waist and let his head rest against mine.

"This couldn't have happened fifteen years ago, you know."

He look up at me, puzzled.

"No one would dare walk the streets with his arm around another man. Strictly *verboten*. We would have been stoned." He thought that anachronism was funny and laughed a little bit. I whispered into his ear, "It's just as good as licking ass." He poked me in the side for the joke.

We were in the middle of our courtship. A fast and furious meeting a few months ago had held all that promise of possibility. There had been immediate melding of physical needs. There was an agreed on limitation to sexual acts – we were being "safe" – but there was no hindering of physical passion. That was there. It had gotten us through our first times together. But now we were becoming . . . something.

It was time for more conversation than before. There was need for more information. It was a weekend of constant pushing and prodding, probing and presenting. It was working.

We got back to his apartment and went into his bedroom. He automatically turned on his stereo. When he turned around I was sitting on the edge of the bed, waiting. He moved toward me. He made a move to sit beside me, but I stopped him with both my hands on his waist. I brought him over, placing him squarely in front of me. He knew what was going to happen.

He leaned into his jeans. Like everything else about him they smelled clean, fresh from the laundry. I inhaled, then pressed my mouth against the fabric. I could feel his cock grow. As always, he was getting hard fast. He could, unlike me, get there and stay there for hours. One of the many pleasures of his body. One of the very many.

I put my arms around his thighs, the back of my palms met and gently guided his legs a little further apart. This time he wasn't wearing underwear. There was just the denim fabric separating my lips from his now firm erection.

I used my face to move the stiffness back and forth, letting it arc up over his belly till it pointed straight toward his waist. Then my mouth could slide up and down the length and could also feel the fleshy sac of his balls beneath. His hands moved and rested on my head. It was just contact, there was no direction to them. They only wanted to feel something more.

I could bring one of my hands up and grab hold of his zipper. I pulled it down. His cock was positioned perfectly. As soon as the opening was undone it was able to fall out into the free air. The smooth, soft skin pressed against my forehead now. I knew better than to go there right away.

Instead my tongue dug further into his jeans and sought out his balls. Even they, even now, tasted like a clean shower. I lapped at them, as I had been before I was amazed at how hairy they were. Not just that, but I loved how thick and wiry that hair was.

I got the two of them out of the fly, they hung over the zipper. I washed them hurriedly. I thought of my cats, the way they enthusiastically cleaned their coats. That was me, ardently covering every one of his hairs with my tongue.

He wasn't having too much of that. In a few minutes he pulled back. Now his hands that had been so passively stretched on my head grabbed hold of me. He positioned himself a bit and then lunged. I suppose I could have fought his cock's attack on my mouth – if I had wanted to.

Instead I opened my jaws and let the entire length of it enter as far as it wanted. My tongue now was moving against his silken shaft. He plunged in and out, holding me still, my body wasn't resisting. When he understood my compliance, his hands began to roam and reached down to search out my nipples through my shirt.

He was usually so calm in his motions, but there were moments like this when that part of him wasn't very apparent. The cock was actually assaulting me, it would uncaringly batter against the back of my throat. His hands weren't kind, they were scratching at me and, even through the shirt, there were sensations of quick pain from his grabbing mingled in with the pleasure.

I suddenly pushed back. There was spit drooling out of the corners of my mouth. I wiped it off with my sleeve. I could see a momentary pang of anger in his expression. Just as pain had mixed with pleasure for me, now some kind of aggravation was merging with his lust.

"I want us both undressed," I said.

I started to unbutton my shirt, but he wasn't ready for that yet. He pressed down on me until we were both sprawled over the covers of his bed. He pressed his chest against mine, put his open mouth on my lips, let his tongue explore inside there for a while. His hands kept up a restless search. First they went to my crotch, then they slid up onto my chest, again looking for my nipples, but now they were easier in their explorations, less frantic when they found their goal.

I spread my legs to let his torso fall between them. I could feel the hard erection pressing against my crotch.

Somehow in all this, without losing my focus on the kissing and the sensation of his hardon between my legs, I was able to pull open my shirt and lift up his. There was a quick, electric sensation of flesh meeting bare flesh. My own hands were doing the prospecting now. They found his tits, wonderful firm little nubs on a flat expanse of bare chest. I had them both in my hands, and that meant I won. That was one thing that made all the difference in our sexual jockeying. I had learned the first time and I had tested it every other time since.

A loud moan escaped him. I shoved only a little but it was enough to make him roll over me slowly enough that my hands didn't lose their grip. I moved down and took one of his nipples into my mouth. I played with it with my tongue first, only occasionally biting. Then I covered the whole of it and sucked hard, gnawing through lip-covered teeth as I did it.

He was writhing beneath me. His hips lifted up. Then they'd collapse under him and squirm from side to side. But he wouldn't ever move so much that he threatened the sensations of my mouth and his tits.

He let my hand wander over his exposed stomach. As always, I was amazed by how hard it was. It was as though that smooth surface had been professionally stretched over his muscles. There wasn't an ounce of spare flesh there, or anywhere else. I would tease him by playing with his other nipple for a bit, but only a short while. Then I would skate my palm down his chest, over his belly, and into his crotch where his cock would be ever hard.

I suddenly released him. His face was frozen in an expression that could only be described as fear – the fear I wouldn't go on. "I told you, let's undress."

Neither of us left the bed, but both slithered out of our clothes and were ready at the same time to crawl between covers. We immediatley embraced, letting our legs twine around each other, our arms clasped around our backs, the kissing resumed.

In the middle of all of it I could feel his hard cock pressing against my stomach and I could feel our balls pushed together, the two hairy surfaces rubbing softly and undulating with the pulsing of our pelvises. But I had started something. I had begun the stimulation of his nipples. He wouldn't begin any new assault, he would only wait for me to resume.

I did. I left his lips and let my mouth trail down over his neck, over one of his smooth, hairless pectoral muscles and then I took his tit back into his mouth.

While I kept up my work on it, I rubbed my erection against his thigh. As hairless as his chest was, his legs were covered with the same thick, wiry hair as his head. Half my weight was resting on him; if he wanted to, he would have had a hard time escaping me. But the insistent pressure of his one free hand on my shoulder proved that escape was the last thing in his mind.

I let my own free hand move down to his crotch. I played with the full feeling balls, so tightly wrapped in his scrotal skin and so beautifully adorned by his pubic hair. My fingertips ran over the surface of his sac while my mouth kept at its work.

Finally I grabbed hold of his cock. My hand enveloped the part of it just beneath the swollen head. I began to masturbate him. I loved the sensation of it as it seemed to unbelievably harden even more. Moans began to sound, breaking free from his throat as though they hadn't any permission. I kept it up for minutes, absorbed in the one small nipple in my mouth and the one big, hard cock in my hand, aware of my thoughts and paying close attention to his breathing.

That was the clue, I had learned that. The telltale signs began to show with its increased speed. His chest began to expand and contract more vigorously. The head of his cock got larger, bursting with even more blood.

His hand tried to push mine away. It would happen soon. He started to struggle with me, desperate, it seemed, to prolong it all. But I was working at a fever pitch now, I was pumping with my palm and chewing with my teeth, knowing that I was going to get my reward soon, I only increased the tempo.

The moans got louder, he lost all control of his breathing, and then, quickly, his cock began to pump out waves of cum onto his belly, one surge so violent it splattered against my head all the way up on his chest.

We didn't stop. I moved up and straddled his abdomen. My own balls were sitting on his now, the hair of both of them meshing together. His mouth was open wide as he looked at me, his hands reached up and – more gently now – found my chest.

"Come all over me," he whispered with the husky sounds of sex reverberating in his voice. "Jerk your fat cock and come all over my chest."

It became a litany. I lost track of it, "Come all over me, jerk off your big cock . . ." I could only feel his balls against mine and his hands working on me and my own hand reaching far inside myself and pulling, demanding, insisting, forcing me to . . . Come all over his belly, sending a seemingly endless wave of stuff onto his body.

I collapsed, almost out of breath. My face was in his pillow beside his. My own chest was heaving now. His arms were strong and calm as they went around me and embraced. I could feel the rapidly cooling liquids on our bodies making me feel wonderfully sleazy and covered with sex.

In a few minutes we were both more relaxed. He got up from underneath me and climbed off the bed to retrieve the inevitable towel. He used it to wipe up the cum that was still on each of us, doing me first, almost lovingly swathing my balls and receding cock. Then he finished with himself. The whole time he had that great smile on his face, the one I'd always loved so much.

"Pure bliss," he pronounced, flopping back onto the bed with me.

"Not even close," I said with a mock tone of severity. "Don't you remember what comes next?"

"You're going to do it?" He wasn't displeased or shocked, but his voice let me know he thought my promise hadn't been one he'd taken seriously.

"Of course," I answered. I got up and went to my suitcase. I put it on top of his bureau and opened it, extracting a quart bottle of the lotion I'd brought with me. I held it up, proof of my intent.

"You'd complained about your skin getting dry." The winter and the way central heating left a body's surface so scaley had been a long conversation between us. "I told you I had the perfect answer.

"And safe too," he replied, a tone of sarcasm in his voice.

"And safe too," I agreed, refusing to give in to him. It would have been a dangerous conversation to continue. There were too many parallels between winter and The Pestilence. I was aware of too many of them, at least.

"Roll over." He turned onto his stomach just as I had commanded. He spread his arms and legs out, leaving himself splayed before my eyes. I had to close them. The sight was, in some ways, too beautiful.

I knelt between his open legs and, remembering all the little suggestions about massage I'd ever heard, carefully warmed the first dollup of lotion in my palms. Only when I could feel no sensation of the liquid's cool, I spread the first dose over his shoulder.

He didn't have a gym-built body. His was natural tone, accentuated by youth. I let the oil lubricate my movements as I kneaded his shoulders. Then, my hands moved down to his waist. I remembered that the slower you went, the more intense the feeling the person got. I forced myself to concentrate on minute areas of his body, using my thumbs to grind into his flesh and letting them stay in that one spot to create the most effective result.

I had him groaning in minutes. I began the repetitive runs up and down his spine. Beginning at his neck, I'd push as hard as I could, making sure there was plenty of lotion, and the side of my hand would dig a path all the length of his back, lifting up only to stop at the beginning of the crack of his ass.

Over and over again, my hand made the trip from top to bottom. It was time for more lotion. I heated it up again in my palms and now went to work on the globes of his ass. His body, front and back, was marble white and unblemished by hair other than the strands that escaped from his armpits. But as soon as you got to his waist, there was a thick coating of the dark rug that continued all the way down to his ankles.

I pawed at his buttocks and marveled at their firmness. A few years ago I would have . . . But now I just kept up my digging at his flesh. There were times when my hands would move in a certain way and the two heaps of flesh would part, giving me an unobstructed view of the long, black line of hair in the cleft of his ass and the target – the inviting, the alluring, the beckoning, *the forbidden* . . .

I'd let the buttocks move back together again and force myself to ignore the wetness in my mouth. I moved now, kneeling at his side. Using more lotion I began on first one of his thighs, then worked the other. They were his pride, his legs. They should have been. They were precisely the kind that made writers talk about "roped tendons" and "woven sinews" and god knows what else. His body was so lean that you could see the hardness of each individual muscle, there was no fatty covering to keep my hands from being able to discern each of them. If I'd remembered my anatomy lessons I could have given them their proper names.

But the touch and the knowledge that he was drifting off into pleasure was more than enough for now. More than enough.

I reached a foot. I had to use double amounts of lotion. The dry skin soaked the stuff up. I worked it carefully, letting my fingers find and massage each of his toes separately. Remembering my lessons to linger, to pay individual attention to each part of his body.

When I'd finished both feet I carefully motioned for him to

turn over. He did it languidly, as though the exertion of rolling over would break some carefully constructed mood he was frightened of losing.

He had an angelic smile on his face, a lazy one, not the boyishly charming one that was usual for him. His limbs weren't carefully arranged now, they seemed almost liquid as they flopped out away from the center of his torso.

I began all over again, climbing onto his belly now, I worked his hands first. Again giving each finger its carefully due reward. Then his palms, his forearms, his biceps. When I moved onto his chest, always remembering to keep the lotion free flowing, he suddenly sucked in air. He was waiting for the contact on his nipples again, waiting for me to touch the conspiratorial buttons. But I refused, knowing that the intense work I did on the rest of his body would more than equally entice him. I shifted my body to let my hands move down to the hard belly I admired. When I moved, I freed his once again hard cock to bob over his pubic bush.

He was ready again. I loved it. His eyes were closed, I saw when I looked up. The smile was still there, that indistinct smile, the one that reflected his personal pleasure, not his seductive charms.

I moved further down, now massaging his abdomen and the restarting of his body hair. But, just as I had avoided his nipples, now I refused to touch his cock or balls, carefully moving around them. I went for his thighs. They were, if anything, more handsome in the front than they had been in the back. The lines of his muscles moved in waves away from his center, they gave an impression of his being bowlegged, but he wasn't. It was just the hard outlines of his strength that created the illusion.

Only when I had reached the top of his feet did he seem to begin to stir. His hips moved, lifted up a bit, then slid to one side. His hands started to grip hold of the sheets beneath them. He was getting ready.

I took a final dose of lotion and crawled back up between his legs. With one oozy hand I took his hard cock. With the other, I reached underneath and found the place where the two mounds of his ass met.

I started pumping again, but this time my other hand was travelling up and down his cleft. His legs lifted up, his feet each rested on one of my own thighs to give me clear access. Only the tips of my fingers were touching his ass. They ran up and down the widely exposed line of it, each trip they hit against his hole, each time sending a kind of shiver through his whole body.

In no time at all there was no way to decide if his body's frissons were from that most intimate contact or from the impending orgasm. I watched his hands clutching the sheets even harder, saw his muscles contracting now. His stomach sucked itself in. His navel became more prominent as the skin tightened around it. He was heaving again, his chest moving quickly with anxious desperation.

Then he came. Again and again the white cum spurted onto his belly. I kept my hand clamped on his cock as he shot, loving the feel of it and my fantasies of its cause.

He was gone far away for awhile. I let him have his personal journey. I waited patiently and content. In a few minutes he opened his eyes and lifted his arms up. I leaned down into his embrace.

Food seemed an intrusion into what was going on, but it was insistent in its demands. We gave in. The shower was perfunctory. We joked a bit, soaped each other up and rinsed together, but we were both drained of playful energy right now. Just a couple guys getting cleaned up for a date . . . with each other.

We dressed and went back out into the winter night. It had gotten dark. The wind was biting and we both shrunk up our shoulders as though a military pose could fight off the freezing weather.

We had to go a few blocks before we got to the restaurant. A friend of his worked there; we got one of his tables. We ordered a drink. He smiled, "I'm already like jelly. I hardly need this."

We sipped the drinks and began to talk. It was Negotiation Time. It was somehow understood that these visits of mine were beginning to approach regularity. Something was going to happen. The little comments had already been made. I was content in the country and had no intentions of moving. He was only 24, back in school and keeping open all his options about moving away once he got his degree.

It was a simple conversation, really. We'd both been clear. We were both infatuated with one another – at least infatuated. There was distance involved and it was enough distance that it assured much more time separated than not. Jobs, futures, other concerns – and time together.

"You want it?" I said once that was clearly what we were talking about.

"Sure," the boyish charm got turned on. Then off. "I think."

I felt myself tense. Rejection wasn't going to be easy to take this time. "Why do you just think?"

"I feel ... strange about you. That you've done all those things. Not just all the fast lane stuff, the baths, the clubs. But I know you have ... games you like to play. You told me, but you don't do it with me. I guess, maybe, I'm interested. But your experiences, your fantasies, they seem to be things I can't match." In a Time of Epidemic.

I shook my head, not knowing how to tell him ... "I'm very happy with you. Our sex is good."

He was serious. "How can you be? I mean, it's one thing to not know any more than this, but ..."

"Today?" I insisted. "You don't think that was good."

He paused over that. "I guess ... I mean, I know. Yes, it was good. But what happens inside your head? I mean, what would you want to do? I have no idea what you're used to."

I took hold of my drink. I looked at it for a while. I was happy to have it suddenly. "There's a danger in all this. You know, most people go through years of relating to one another and not knowing what they're thinking. If I tell you what's going on I might scare you.

"Look, the things you call games, they're highly tuned duets, they're things that are loaded with symbols that both people know about, understand."

"Yeah, I know that. I feel strange because – for me, just for me – they're too contrived. I can't get into all the costumes, all the scenarios." He paused. "I told a friend about you. I told him about the stuff you used to do in the Mineshaft, all the trips, the S & M, the stuff that used to happen." Before The Devastation.

He smiled. "He wondered how I could get it on with you, told me I wasn't very imaginative. I'm not creative. I like sex, I like our sex. I just keep wondering if it's all right with you."

I started to talk, trying to be careful. "Look, if you and I spent all our time worrying that all we're doing is jerking off and we only paid attention to all the things we weren't doing and weren't enjoying, it would be a disaster. I agree with you. But . . ." I took a deep breath, leaned across the table and spoke more, now in a lower voice.

"Look, here's what's going on in my mind while we have sex. That's really what you want to know. Okay, this is it, step by step, this afternoon.

"We went into the bedroom and I sat on the edge of the bed. You turned and I pulled you over. I slipped your cock out of your pants. Your hard dick stabbed into my mouth. You were – at that moment – someone who wasn't going to be stopped. You were *fucking* my mouth. You became some piece of rough trade ready, willing and able to push that thing of yours down my throat.

"Then we got on the bed. You were on top of me. It became a contest. I had to get your tits and stop you or you were going to win, you were going to shove that hard cock down my throat again and gag me for the rest of the day. I got to your tits. I won.

"Then you were mine. All mine. My tongue and my mouth got you. You might as well have been in bondage, I could have pulled out all the rope in America and you couldn't have moved any more than you did. It was my trip, my control. I got you to come, I *made* you come, you were fighting it and it didn't make any difference.

"I climbed on top of you, a victor. I jerked my cock off in front of your face. You wanted to suck it – I saw that. You *wanted* to. But I kept it from you. Maybe if you'd begged, *maybe* I would have let you.

"I can't begin to tell you all the things about massaging you . . ."

"Try." He interrupted, his eyes were serious, studying me.

"You're right. My mind goes wild sometimes. It's the experiences I can conjure up from my past and the pleasures that I'm getting right now. All of it coming together. At one moment you were some stud slave getting oiled up to be presented to some masters. At another you were a fighter getting relaxed after a big battle and *needing* your buddy to help you out, cool you down. Then you were this perfect specimen, some kind of rich and spoiled young master getting taken care of. Then you were a kid, a real young kid, no hair on your chest, maybe you were in the locker room and getting a rub down, who knows? Maybe I was some dirty old man in the park, trying to get you to go further, but you were young, very young . . ."

"You like that, don't you? The age thing?"

"Yeah, I like it a lot." Dangerous ground here. "I never used to notice these age differences. Really. I never quite understood what they were about, why it made some of the older guys I did it with so excited and so very hot and bothered. Now I do.

"It's part of age, part of getting older. Your skin feels different. Your muscles aren't the same as mine. I'm not getting crazy about growing older, but it makes me feel . . . the difference between us. You taste different, for Christ's sake. I spend time thinking about that and enjoying that nowadays, I never used to. But you taste different. Your sweat tastes different . . ."

"Good?"

"Very good."

Our food came them. The friendly waiter had gotten huge portions for us. The meal went on, he'd every once in a while ask another question, he'd go back to one of my fantasies.

"Would you really like to be a coach to me?"

"Look, I promise you, this thing's going to go on longer than this horrible winter. When it's over, we're going to the beach. You're going to get into the tightest speedo known and I'm going to spend the whole day in the sun watching you in it, looking at the contours of your cock and balls and checking out how jealous the rest of the crowd is that you're with me. When we get back to our room, I'm going to give you that rub down, take care of your skin, make sure you don't get a sunburn, then you're going to show me just how much you appreciate all the attention, you're going to show me a lot of appreciation."

I smiled. I liked that one.

"Clothes do it for you, don't they?" He was back to studying again.

"I'll tell you something, one of the things that I get into is watching you every time you get undressed. The great question in mind is whether or not you're wearing jockey shorts. Now, I have to warn you about them. You were all concerned about not setting things up too tightly, not getting them to be too mechanical. Okay. We won't do the grand scenarios. But you haven't told me yet that there's anything I can't do.

"One day you're going to strip down and I'm going to see that young body in just jockey shorts and you're going to look at me just the wrong way – or maybe it's the right way – and you're going to be across my knees so fast you're not going to know what happened to you. Your butt's going to be slapped like you can't remember it being done before. Then . . ."

"Yeah?"

"Then I'm going to jerk you off like you won't believe."

"Just cause I'm wearing jockey shorts?"

"Of course," I leaned back now, feeling better, feeling more in stride, "it might be that my mind won't be there. It might have made you *very* young. I could just be nice to you, like you were some scared little altar boy – I think of you that way sometimes – and I'll sit you down and reach inside the briefs and pull out your cock. I jerk it off nice and easy and slow while we kiss and talk and I tell you it's going to be okay, all of it's going to be okay."

The check came. We paid it and started to walk back to his apartment.

"All that, just from jerking off?" He said it suddenly as we got to his door. We moved quickly to get inside, I didn't answer until we were safely in the entryway.

"Just that from jerking off, if you want to be so dumb about it."

"Dumb? It's not dumb. They're all the things we're not doing." He had pushed the button for the elevator. He turned to look at me more directly. "Don't you want to fuck me?"

More than you'll ever know.

The elevator door opened and we walked in. The car took us to his floor. We got to his apartment and automatically went to his bedroom. The stereo went on. I spread out over the bed. It had been often enough, authentic enough, he simply undressed. I watched him. He was taking his time, folding his clothes. They weren't going to be needed again tonight and the next morning he'd have to dress for school.

Nonchalantly, I dragged my own off and let them scatter on the floor. Another good reason not to live in the same city. He was compulsively neat; I was compulsively sloppy. On a few weekends he could take it; I knew he'd go crazy if it were more often than that.

When I was naked I looked over and he was standing there – in his jockey shorts. The front of them was stained wet. I stared at the soaked spots. "Thought you'd like to see what I thought of your stories," he said. A little smile of self-deprecation came over his face. "I was hard all through dinner."

"That good?"

"That good," he said. He came over to me and laid his body on top of mine. We kissed. "Do I get a spanking yet?"

"Not right now. Soon enough. Got to keep something in the background to make sure you keep that little edge of tension, the worry. It makes things happen better, more spontaneously." We kissed again.

"I have a surprise for you. You wanted to watch that movie on tv, right?"

"Right."

He jumped up and put on a robe, then disappeared into the front of the apartment. He came back with two bottles of champagne in his hand and two fluted glasses. "A touch of class, fits the time." It was the name of the movie.

He popped the cork and then filled the glasses. We playfully and silently toasted one another. He switched off the stereo then turned on the tv.

For the rest of the night we stayed there, both of us naked. I felt the luxuriant touch of his nude balls as they pressed against me. Our hands would roam over our bodies, our cocks would move purposelessly from hard to soft, the conversation moved in spurts while the film went on.

We were tired. A long day, a big meal, and now champagne. There was more than a half of the second bottle left. I suddenly reached over and poured some in his deep navel. Then I leaned down and sucked it out of him bringing out some reaction that was more than just pleasure, less than a giggle.

He smoothed a palm on the side of my head. "You really can get it on this way, can't you? It must be hard. All the things you're not doing."

"There you go again," I said. He was pushing.

"But you told me, the friends, the people you knew, the . . ."

The Plague.

I lifted up the bottle. "Look at this. What do you see?"

He was puzzled, he couldn't answer.

"You have two choices, just two. There's no grey, there's no option. This bottle of champagne is half full, or it's half empty. That's your choice. I've spent too long, way too long, deciding it was half empty, that there was nothing to do but what was missing. It'a pretty horrible way to look at life and sex. But that's what it amounts to.

"I can go back to nights in the baths and a string of anonymous men with beautiful bodies and willing assholes and I can sit here and tell you what torture it is not to fuck you every time I get a hard on.

"Or," I broke into a theatrical voice, cutting the hard edge of my feelings, "I can look at this body and feel this cock you have and I can decide the bottle is half full. The champagne has all these bubbles left. It's got a lot of effervescence. It is going to keep us happy and celebrating." Through the Pestilence.

"Most people don't ever get to taste champagne in their lives. I get to taste you, I get to imagine your skin and think about the dick of yours that never seems to go down. I get to suck on it for a while at least . . ."

"No ingestion," he was joking now.

". . . and then I get to feel it, feel all the power and the strength of your young body while it shoots and your balls pull up hard against your body, and . . ."

"I'm the full half of your bottle of champagne?"

"And I'm going to do everything possible to see that it lasts and lasts for years and gives more and more pleasure."

"Sounds pretty good, doesn't it?" He took the bottle from my hand and poured two more glasses. We did our silent toast again. But he broke it at the last minute, "To life."

Our hands froze the glasses in front of our lips, "To love," I dared to say it.

"To a long future," he answered.

"And lots of champagne.'

Then we drank, and with the wine still in our mouths, we kissed.

Somehow the glasses got to the bedside table. Somehow there were arms and hands, hard cocks and great joy, and somehow the night ended with great peace.

CONTRIBUTORS NOTES

PHIL ANDROS is the legendary pen name of Samuel Steward. His life spans decades of gay writing including some of the most important and (in all ways) seminal gay erotica. His most recent book, as Samuel Steward, is *Murder is Murder is Murder*, a mystery published by Alyson Publications.

DAVID BARTON-JAY is the (in)famous author of *The Enema As An Erotic Art And Its History*, as well as the writer of a monthly column in *Manscape*. He is now at work on a new opus on spanking. We assume he is as busy with his research on that topic as he is with its actual writing.

MAX EXANDER lives in San Francisco. He is the author of *Safestud* (Alyson Publications) and *Mansex* (Gay Sunshine Press). The story included in this volume is adapted from a portion of *Safestud*.

EDWIN CLARK (TOBY) JOHNSON resides in San Antonio, Texas where, in addition to being a writer, he is a gay community organizer and psychotherapist. Johnson is author of *The Myth of the Great Secret: A Search for Spiritual Meaning in the Face of Emptiness* (Morrow) and *In Search of God in the Sexual Underworld* (Morrow). He did research and counseling with teenage runaways in San Francisco as a part of a federally-sponsored project. He is currently working on a novel.

MACH has published over nine million words of adult fiction, mostly heterosexual. He was founding editor of a currently successful gay magazine and has a graduate degree in film.

ROBIN METCALFE was born and raised in Atlantic Canada; he now lives in Halifax, Nova Scotia. He's worked as a sleeping-car porter on the Halifax-Montreal run of VIA Canada for the last ten years, was active in gay politics on the local and national levels, and writes news stories for *The Body Politic* – all that and still finding time to write poetry. He is now writing full time and publishes regularly in gay periodicals in Canada, the United States, Australia, Sweden and the United Kingdom. Writing erotic fiction, he says, "allows me to indulge two passions, for gay sex and the English language."

FRANK MOSCA is the author of *All American Boys* (Alyson Publications), a young adult novel. He's published short fiction in *Mandate* and *First Hand*. At the moment he is working on a screenplay and some semi-technical manuals. He was born in Massachusetts but has spent his adult life in California where he was coordinator of the Claremont Gay Student Union in the early seventies. Presently, he volunteers as a hotline monitor for a local gay center and helps facilitate a new gay youth group.

JOHN PRESTON is the author of *Mr. Benson* (Alternate Publishing). His Alyson books include *Franny, the Queen of Provincetown, I Once Had a Master and Other Tales of Erotic Love.* The first three volumes of his male action series, The Mission of Alex Kane, have been released, a fourth is on its way. With Frederick Brandt, he wrote *Classified Affairs: A Gay Man's Guide to the Personal Ads.*

ERIC ROFES is a writer and community activist living in Provincetown, Massachusetts. He is the author of *I Thought People Like That Killed Themselves: Lesbians, Gay Men and Suicide* (Grey Fox Press) and has contributed articles to *Gay Community News, The Advocate, Bay Windows,* and various other publications. Alyson Publications has just published *Socrates, Plato, and Guys Like Me: Confessions of a Gay Schoolteacher,* a book about Rofes's experiences as a closeted gay schoolteacher. This is his first piece of published erotic fiction.

MARTY RUBIN is better known in South Florida as the infamous "Bike Daddy," whose *Weekly News* column of social and political satire and gay sleaze has outraged his local readers for the past eight years. He has appeared in *Drummer* and *Chicago Gay Life* and is a regular contributor to

Manscape. Mr. Rubin's unfulfilled dream is to be able to devote himself exclusively to writing. He is presently working on a novel.

TRIPP VANDERFORD is the pen name of Kris Lewallen. A graduate of the University of North Carolina, Kris received his B.A. in French, which he insists is not a pun. He is a regular contributor to *Advocate Men*, *Blueboy*, *Manscape* and *Torso* magazines and resides in New York City.

GEORGE WHITMORE is a novelist (*The Confessions of Danny Slocum*) and a freelance journalist based in New York.

T.R. WITOMSKI is a frequent (actually – permanent) contributor to magazines and newspapers (some gay; some even more reprehensible), though he denies it. He specializes in sitting around his Toms River, New Jersey home, smoking cigarettes, drinking Budweiser, and making jokes at the expense of others. He is unable to get himself a real job. Authorities agree that the only way to stop him is to drive a stake through his heart.

DARRELL YATES RIST has committed his life to prurient interests. His investigations have appeared in a range of periodicals from *Christopher Street* to *Forum*. Among his most perverse endeavors was scripting and filming Nancy Reagan at the White House then dishing her on the pages of *Harper's Magazine*.

Other books of interest from Alyson Publications

☐ **ONE TEENAGER IN TEN: Writings by gay and lesbian youth,** edited by Ann Heron, $4.00. One teenager in ten is gay; here, twenty-six young people tell their stories: of coming to terms with being different, of the decision how – and whether – to tell friends and parents, and what the consequences were.

☐ **SWEET DREAMS,** by John Preston, $5.00. Who says heroes can't be gay? Not John Preston. In his new Alex Kane series, he has created a gay alternative to The Destroyer and The Executioner – a crusader against homophobia, whose only weakness is other men.

☐ **$TUD,** by Phil Andros; introduction by John Preston, $7.00. Phil Andros is a hot and horny hustler with a conscience, pursuing every form of sex – including affection – without apology, yet with a sense of humor and a golden rule philosophy. When Sam Steward wrote these stories back in the sixties, they elevated gay fiction to new heights; today they remain as erotic and delightful as ever.

☐ **THE SPARTAN,** by Don Harrison, $6.00. In the days of the first Olympics, gay relationships were a common and valued part of life. *The Spartan* tells the story of a young athlete and his adventures in love and war, providing a vivid picture of classical Greece, the early Olympics, and an important part of our history.

☐ **REFLECTIONS OF A ROCK LOBSTER: A story about growing up gay,** by Aaron Fricke, $5.00. When Aaron Fricke took a male date to the senior prom, no one was surprised: he'd gone to court to be able to do so, and the case had made national news. Here Aaron tells his story, and shows what gay pride can mean in a small New England town.